A Year Less Three Days

Alyx Jae Shaw

When Lias' wife was kidnapped, all his skills as a woodsman couldn't save her—or himself. Captured, sold repeatedly to different masters, Lias endures abuse, torture, and worse. By the time his latest master buys him, Lias is little more than an animal.

At times, Necromis, a knight of the Order of the White Bear, would like nothing more than to oblige his aggravating new charge, but one thing stays his deadly hand: Lias is his last hope. The day of reckoning is coming, and there's only one way out of this bargain—capture the heart of a broken slave, or Necromis' soul will forever belong to Bonecracker.

(This title was previously published but has been revised.)

Arian Derwydd Books, LLC

https://arianderwyddbooks.com/

DEDICATION

To Caz M, for my continued survival and her gifts of encouragement.
To Pointy, who says "Call me if you need to" and means it.
To Myc Cook, whom I once rescued from a herd of Aztec Battle-Sloths.

Chapter One

Eighteen months ago. It had only been eighteen months, but it had been whole centuries. Lias could still play the whole story over in his mind, like some brilliant fairy tale gone horribly wrong.

Once upon a time, there had been a woodsman, who lived in the forest with his beautiful wife Elyssa and three little daughters. They'd been poor, but they'd been happy. The woodsman would cut trees, and sometimes his daughters would follow him and pick berries and flowers and gather herbs and what fruit and roots they could find. In the evenings, they would return home to their cottage, and eat dinner, sing, tell stories, and laugh. Sometimes, his wife would play the harp — an extravagant instrument for a woodsman's wife, but she had once been a lady in a manor house until she decided she far preferred the simple life in the woods near the stream, where the sun shone on the wildflowers outside her door. Her father had not been delighted with her choice, but he agreed to put her happiness over what was proper. And the woodsman knew that if ever he mistreated his beloved, he would be run down like a stag by a dozen hunters, her father leading the pack.

Then she died.

Lias was glad her father was visiting when she did, so that he could see her passing was not her husband's fault. But as she died, Lias and her father Sir Blackmoore both had the strange feeling her passing was anything but natural. Sir Blackmoore brought in the best healers and scryers he could find to determine what had happened to her, but none could say. Or were afraid to say. Sir Blackmoore was a powerful man in this area and not without numerous enemies. A pointed finger could start a war.

Sir Blackmoore appointed his granddaughters a nanny, and life went on, still good, but not as happy. After a year had passed, Lias married the nanny, a woman by the name of Merdine. Then tragedy struck once more. Sir

Blackmoore was killed when his horse panicked and ran off a bridge, plunging both of them into a shallow, stony river.

Life became harder without the assistance of the children's grandfather, and it seemed the sun shone less bright on their tiny home in the woods. Then, one night, Lias came home out of the rain to find his children crying and terrified, his wife gone, and a man he only knew in passing standing in his small house. His name was Broadin, a man from the village a few miles away, and he looked as if he had been in a violent fight.

"What happened?" asked Lias, his three small daughters clutching him and weeping.

"Traders," said Broadin. "Merdine bought a new kettle in town and asked me to bring it here for her as she had too much to carry already. By the time I arrived with the iron kettle, they had taken her."

"Traders?" exclaimed Lias. "Would we have not heard of them coming up the rivers in their ships?"

"Sir Blackmoore manned the watch to keep the traders at bay. Since he died…"

Lias looked down at his crying children, then to Broadin. "Will you watch them for a while for me?"

Broadin's jaw dropped. "Lias, you do not mean to go after these men!"

"I cannot simply allow them to take her and sell her like an animal! She is my wife! Even if she were not, I could not leave her to such a fate! I must try!"

"Lias, you're *mad*," said Broadin.

"Be that as it may. Will you mind my children?"

"I will, but what shall I tell them if you do not come back?"

Lias looked down at their small faces staring up at him, all dark with eyes of polished jade, like their mother.

"I *will* be back."

* * *

Lias shook his head, abruptly waking from his half-sleep, hearing the quiet clank of his chains. Oh, he had been a fool; a heroic fool, but a fool nonetheless. He had been captured within moments of coming across their vessel. After all, these traders lived the roaming life of warriors, stealing and pillaging and selling to earn their way when there were no wars to fight. Lias was a woodsman, and while he was strong, trees rarely fought back. He'd been caught and chained and sold in under an hour, and the man who bought him had not been pleased with his purchase.

Lias had wanted nothing more than to find and save his wife, and the moment he was let off his chain, he was gone. He was recaptured, chained, and sold again, this time to a stonecutter who needed a strong back to help him in the quarry. Again, Lias ran. Again, Lias was caught. Again, he was sold. His price kept dropping, and his masters changed from tradesmen to men so depraved that Lias had no words to describe them.

Now, eighteen months later, he had been shackled, raped, beaten, tortured, used as a live moving target, bearbait, dogbait, and broken down into a man who no longer truly recalled what had ever made him leave home.

He looked up at the chains that held him, scarcely able to lift his own head. He was shackled in a standing position, naked, the blood drying on his back from his latest whipping. His strength was gone. There would be no fleeing his next master. Lias was at the end of his life, and he knew it. He would hang in these chains until he was sold or he died. His reputation as a fighter and a runner had doomed him. At least as the slave of the stonecutter, there would have been some dignity, but it would not be a tradesman coming to purchase him now. At best, it would be a dog breeder, looking for cheap meat and bones to give to the hounds.

He wondered how his children were doing and if they were still in the house in the woods. Most likely, they were living with Broadin, learning to set the sand casts for the items he made. It would not be a bad life for them. The gods above knew there were far worse.

The door to his dark cell opened, and someone walked in to put a cloth sack over his head. That meant someone was coming to look at him, and they did not want him spitting at the customer. Lias managed a half-hearted growl.

"Mind your manners for once," muttered the attendant.

Lias was doused with a bucket of cold water to clean off the worst of the mess, then left to hang a little while longer. Lias' long, ragged, black hair hung in his face, dripping and stinking like the rest of him. Honestly, who would want him?

Then a scent entered his world of stink and pain, a fragrance like the sun on the flowers in Elyssa's garden. He raised his head, sniffing. What ghost was this, coming to him in the darkness of his miserable cell? Was he dying? He heard the rustle of fine cloth, and he sniffed again. Surely, they were not bringing a lady into this pit. Then he heard the voice of the slave-trader.

"My lord, surely, there is nothing down here that will appeal to you."

Good grief, was that swishing flower-smell a *man*? The sound of a quiet and definitely masculine voice confirmed his suspicion.

"Fine gems are often found in the mire."

"My lord, he's no treasure. He bites."

The customer laughed quietly. "Does he, now? Could it have anything at all to do with the chains or the whippings? You've beaten him half to death. Look at these marks. This was once a perfectly serviceable man. You've turned him into hanging meat."

"T'was not I, my lord. It was the eleven masters before me in the last few months who did it. I've handled slaves with the demons of the underworld in them before, but Bonecracker himself lives in *that* one."

"Does he indeed?" The voice was soft, amused. Almost as if this man knew something that others did not.

Lias felt a hand on his shoulder, checking his bones, his muscles, feeling for any breaks or deformities that would keep him from working. A tradesman? Here? No, not with

7

that much perfume on him. A merchant, then. Someone looking for a body to haul heavy items.

"He seems sound. I'll take him."

"My lord, *please* reconsider. I've some very pretty boys from the Seven Isles just in this…"

"If I wanted a pampered little snot who thinks he's far better than he is simply because he is purpose-bred and can sing out his lineage on command, then I would have bought one. This man pleases me. Brats do not. Clean him up and deliver him by evening meal. Why does he have a bag over his head?"

"He spits, too, my lord."

The man sighed. "Remove the bag. I wish to see his eyes."

The merchant did, and Lias saw his new master for the first time. The image was rather daunting. Perfume and fine silks aside, this man was the tallest he had ever seen, with eyes the colour of green elven-fire. His shoulders were broad, and his bearing was that of one born to the ruling classes. Beneath his silken robes, which were embroidered with images of roaring bears, was chainmail, clinking with a faint, delicate sound. Across his back was a sword, and Lias knew what he was looking at was a knight of the kingdom to the north. What was it called? It had always seemed so far away from his little house in the woods, more like a fairy tale than a real place. Huh. A knight. He was going to belong to a knight.

Why would a *knight* want him?

Lias stared at the man with a sort of dull curiosity, too weary and broken to do much more. He'd never seen a knight. He wished his daughters were here. They would have been out of their minds with excitement to see a real knight.

No. Not here. Anywhere but here.

Ixander. That was the name of the kingdom. Ixander.

"His eyes are clear. Good."

8

Lias felt a faint trace of his inner fire flare up as the tall man took his face between his hands. Perhaps Bonecracker did live within him. It was the only logical explanation for why he lunged and snapped at the man's face. The knight shoved him back, and the trader popped the bag over Lias' head once more.

"My lord, I did warn you."

The man sighed. "Indeed, you did. But I stand by my decision. What is his price?"

"Three baenea, my lord."

Three baenae? He really *had* come down in price. At the start of this adventure, he'd fetched two hundred reids. Gone from the price of a fine horse to the cost of a strawberry sweetie on a summer's day. The knight made a quiet sound of amusement.

"So you do not charge extra for the biting."

"We try to discourage that in the slaves we sell. If we could tame him, he would be worth far more, but he won't respect the whip."

"Just clean him up as well as you are able and send him to my house. I expect there will be a delivery charge since he cannot travel on his own, and if he could, he would simply head for the furthest land he could reach, in all likelihood."

"The delivery fee will be waived in light of his behaviour. Indeed, I am glad to get him off my hands."

"Very well then. Our business is done."

The knight left. The slave-trader sighed heavily.

"That's a knight of Ixander, so you had better behave. If he wearies of your nonsense, you'll be having warm fantasies about being *back* here hanging in chains."

The chains were released, and Lias dropped to the floor in unspeakable pain. He was half carried, half dragged out of the cell and up a set of cold stone stairs into a small room. He suspected it was a place of torture, judging from some of the implements he saw hanging. It struck him as hilarious in a sick, dark way. Wasn't being a slave torture enough?

9

He was put in a tub and scrubbed down like an animal, no consideration paid to his injuries. The bag was yanked off his head long enough to soak his head and wash his hair, then quickly replaced as he tried to sink his teeth into the trader's face. Lias was uncertain when his habit of biting had begun; certainly not before he was taken from his home. Now, with his hands often shackled, it was his only way of lashing out.

"Here, behave, you," said the trader as he finished rinsing the soap off Lias. "You could show a little gratitude, you know. I didn't have to let him see you. I shouldn't have anyway. With all *your* habits, you'll be back in a week with 'murderer' emblazoned on your back, waiting to be thrown into the pits for the royal bears."

Lias said nothing in response to the man. He had stopped speaking not long after he began biting. He saw no reason to behave like a man after all he had endured. His neck still pained him from when the slave traders caught him that dark night eighteen months ago. What a fool he had been. What an utter laughable fool. Had he really thought that he, a woodcutter, could do battle with and defeat twenty armed traders? Men who filled their bellies and fed their babes by murder and looting? He had been caught in moments, chained down, and when he refused to submit, one of the stinking hairy brutes raped him, just to teach him his place. It would not be the last time he had his body violated. Lias had felt anger before, but nothing like the raging black hatred that filled his brain now, constantly darkening his thoughts and turning his mind to vengeance. The first chance he got, he would kill, and he did not care who.

He was dragged from the bath and dried, then dressed in a clean tunic of cheap cloth. Since he was known to both bite and spit, a piece of heavy rope was forced between his jaws and fixed into place with wire. Some of his wild black hair got tangled into the wire, but there was no care given over that. His hands were bound, but as he was dragged from the large structure where the traders housed their slaves and loaded into the wagon to be delivered, he managed to catch the man in the face with his foot.

This amused one of the two other slaves in the wagon; one an enormous, bearded man who seemed downright jolly. He was in no way restrained and seemed to be looking forward to his destination. Lias had seen slaves like him before — men who had a craft and were highly prized. Often, they were sold repeatedly from one craftsman to the next, and while their lives were hardly settled, they were treated with care and respect, viewed as a valuable tool to share within the circle of craftsmen. He would be going to a familiar place, a hot meal, a warm bed, and an honest day's work, which was more than Lias had.

The second slave was one of the so-called pretty boys from Seven Isles. Lias hated him on sight. He was cute and coiffed and clearly as arrogant as a god. He would have been raised from infancy to play instruments, write, read, sing, dance, to know the etiquette for all occasions, and to be a graceful and elegant pet for his mistress or master. Lias would have liked to force him to eat a mouthful of shit.

"Here, now," said the bearded man. "Let me help you to sit up, there's a grand fellow. Oh, I see they have a bit on you. Been naughty, have you? Let's take this out and have a conversation."

Lias thought the painted pretty boy was going to faint as the bit was removed. The large man set it aside while Lias worked his jaw and shook his head, trying to get the taste of the rope out of his mouth. It tasted the way a dirty horse smelled.

"There now, that's better. What's your name? I'm Carstairs, the glassmaker."

No wonder this man was so highly prized — that was a rare talent to find in a slave.

"Now — why do they have you gagged?" asked Carstairs. "Let me guess — you've a terrible singing voice."

Lias curled his lip slightly. He didn't care what sort of master he got. He had wanted only to save his wife, not to

11

damn himself and leave his children without parents. The 'pretty boy' rolled his eyes and made a 'tsk!' of derision.

"Why are you bothering to talk to that thing? It's barely human. Put the gag back in its mouth, or if you won't, I will."

The young man picked up the gag and intended to shove it into Lias' mouth. Lias lunged, catching the prized and valuable slave's hand. He had managed to get the ball of the thumb, and he made full use of his own strength, biting down as hard as he was able, chewing and shaking his head. Carstairs tried to pull Lias off, but Lias would not release his hold. He simply kept chewing and shaking until he struck gristle and bone. The shrieks of pain from his victim caused the wagon driver to stop his horses and come to the back of the wagon to determine what the commotion was all about.

"Who took off his gag?" the driver demanded.

"I did, and believe me, I'll never do such a fool thing again! He's out of his mind!"

Something was forced into Lias' mouth, and his teeth were made to release the young man's hand.

"He's ruined me!" shrieked the Seven Isles slave. "Look at this! Look at my hand! Get him away! He means to kill me!"

Lias growled as the gag was jammed so forcefully into his mouth, it was surprising his teeth did not break. It was fastened into place by Carstairs as the wagon driver tended to the Seven Isles slave.

"How bad is he?" asked Carstairs.

The wagon driver shook his head. "He'll be fine, but we have to replace him with another. Lady Swennon won't tolerate a mark like *that* on one of her slaves."

"Can't you fix it?" The slave was in near hysterics. "A scar like that will affect my price! What about my hand? Will it work? I don't want to be a common house-slave!"

Carstairs attached a chain that was fastened to the floorboards around Lias' neck. "Your new master won't be pleased with you, my lad," said Carstairs. "Not when he finds himself the owner of a Seven Isles slave."

12

"You mean I have to live under the same roof as that monster?" His blue eyes were large, and his face paint was streaked from tears.

"That's the law!" said the wagon driver. "His master is responsible for any mischief he gets up to. That means he has to pay for your replacement cost, and that means you go to live with him."

The slave began screaming and swearing at Lias in a language Lias did not speak. Soon, his hand was bandaged, and the wagon was underway once more. Carstairs looked to Lias.

"Your life is going to be short and miserable, friend, if they can't get those demons out of you."

Short and miserable? How much more so could it be? His first wife was dead, his second taken, he was bound and stuffed into a wagon like a goat after being beaten, violated, mocked, and tortured, and now this man was lecturing him about his manners. First chance he got, he'd end Carstairs' glassmaking career. He would like to see how well the large man could craft glass with no eyes. Perhaps Bonecracker lived in him after all. If that was true, then Lias saw no reason to tell the demon to depart.

* * *

They arrived before the huge manor house, with its enormous gardens and lawn and grand trappings. Lias knew it a fabulous place of much beauty, although it was difficult to see much of it. The hour was late, the skies were black, and the only chance he had to look at his new home was when the lightning flashed. That, also, was when Lias learned how very far he was from his own little home. The flag waving above the tallest peaks of the house showed the white horse on a field of blue and green, the flag of Ixander. He was in the country of the north.

Lias was taken from the wagon by servants and carried to the house. He was taken upstairs to an ornate chamber, placed on a small, low bed on the floor, chained to a great timber, and left after his gag was removed. The

13

servants made certain they moved well out of the way of him quickly. Clearly, they had been warned.

Lias sat on the bed and looked around. He was in a bedroom, he realized; one that could easily hold his entire house back home. Directly across from him was the bed of whoever claimed this room as their own; a gigantic creation of ebony and gold, draped in golden quilts and fabrics. To the right was an enormous tub of white porcelain, hand-painted with flowers and birds. To his left, an area for dressing, reading, lounging, and entertaining. Lanterns and candles bathed the entire room in a surreal golden glow, and he could not help but think how his daughters would have loved a room like this for their very own. There was even a fireplace with images of rearing horses, running stags, fruiting trees, and eagles carved into it. Instead, they had to make do with one bed for the three of them, and one small room as well.

He wondered what they were doing right now and if their stepmother was even alive.

Lias stayed alone in the room for what seemed like a very long time. Long enough to put significant effort into getting out of his chain, to absolutely no avail. When it became clear he was not going to escape, he tried his aim by pissing on a very valuable tapestry woven of silk, fine wool, and golden thread to form what seemed to be a heraldic crest. Since it was several feet away, this took a great deal of intentional effort.

If he had to live like a bad dog, he was certainly going to behave like one.

Finally, he heard the door open, then close. Footsteps walked across the stone floor, and a man strolled into view. It was the same knight Lias had seen in the slave-trader's warehouse. His new master was no less striking in his own quarters. He removed his cloak, and Lias saw now an impressive river of white hair that went down to the man's knees. The knight placed his cloak on a stand wrought to look like young dragons winding around a sapling, then paused, sniffing. The golden-green eyes narrowed, then

14

shifted to Lias. He stared at him for a long moment, then began removing his gloves.

"I saw that boy you attacked. It will grieve you to know he will keep his thumb."

Lias honestly did not care if the boy kept his thumb or not. He was too wrapped in his bitterness to care about the fates of others. He wanted only for his enslavement to end, one way or another. The knight pulled a bell-rope, and minutes later, a servant appeared.

"Yes, my master?"

"Merrigale, it grieves me to ask you this, but could you see about cleaning my tapestry?"

The older woman stepped forward to examine it, then drew back in horror. "My lord, surely, you have plans of retaliating for this disgusting and disrespectful act?"

"First, I intend to learn if he is sane or not. Then I will reprimand him accordingly."

"We've bears that need feeding," she muttered grimly.

Merrigale, along with two other servants, took the tapestry away to be cleaned. Once they were gone, the tall knight drew something out of a hardened leather case. It was a long tube of tobacco, rolled up into fine rice paper. Lias knew then this man had to be a knight of one of the highest orders; they being the only ones who could afford to smoke their tobacco in such a manner. The knight lit the cigarette with an ember from the fire, then turned to Lias.

"Your disgusting display has done nothing more than create extra work for a servant of whom I am quite fond. If you do not care for your own fate, have a thought for theirs. Now — what is your name?"

Lias turned his back to him and was about to settle onto his bed when a hand grabbed him by his chain, yanked him to his feet, and slammed him repeatedly into a wall. He was dropped to the floor, and lay staring up at the tall man.

"Let me make one thing perfectly clear. In this house, you get no care, or consideration, or kindness, until you earn it. I did not put you in those shackles, but I did take

15

you out of a blackened hole in which they intended to let you die. I do not expect gratitude, but I do expect you to behave like something other than a feral goblin. If this is asking too much, then keep in mind that I am a knight of the highest ranking in this kingdom, and that means I *do indeed* have bears to feed. I will think nothing of splitting open your guts and throwing you to them whilst you are alive to appreciate it if you try my patience once more."

Lias edged away from the man, retreating to his small bed, his blue eyes fixed on his tall master. Lias had been down this path before, and often, in past months. It never ended well.

The man continued to stand over him, smoking. "What is your name?" he asked in a firm, even voice.

Lias cringed slightly, anticipating a blow, waiting for a chance to strike back. The man did not strike him, and that only heightened Lias' fear. He had learned it was the ones who did not strike him who inflicted the worst punishments.

The man stared at him, awaiting an answer. When it became clear there was none coming, he briefly left the room. He returned a few minutes later with a bowl of sliced meat in gravy. Lias sat up, salivating like an animal, unable to contain himself. He was starving, and the sight of food — *good* food, worthy of a table, and not rancid scraps — broke down his carefully erected walls. The knight seated himself on the floor, arranging himself elegantly and out of range of Lias' teeth. He dipped a silver fork into the meat and raised a piece.

"This is how the game is played. If you answer me in a civil manner without biting or spitting or pissing, you may have a piece of meat. If you do not behave in a civil manner, you get nothing. Am I clear?"

He was very clear, but Lias was confused. What game was this? Why was this knight being kind? Was the meat poisoned or tainted in some way? Nothing good ever came of things like this. Lias had learned quickly that there was no such thing as true kindness when one was a slave.

16

"Am I clear?" the man asked sternly.

Lias nodded warily.

"Very good. Now, to begin—what is your name?"

It had been so long since last he spoke that Lias had some difficulty remembering how to do so. "Lias," he finally said in a near-whisper. "I am Lias."

The knight offered Lias a piece of meat on the end of a fork. Like a nervous wolf, Lias moved forward to accept it, closing his lips over the tidbit. It was good. It was *so* good. It was salty and hot and succulent and flavoured with exotic tastes he could not identify, and he swallowed it so fast, he nearly choked. He almost began to cry as he felt a rage well up inside of himself that his own body could betray him so, reducing him to a subservient pet for a piece of meat. But he was so hungry...

"All right, Lias, next question. What are your skills?"

Lias fought to get his emotions under control, battling with anger and grief and humiliation. All the whippings, all the beatings, the assaults, none of them could break him. But a simple bowl of meat had him crawling.

"I was a woodsman. I cut trees and hew them into boards and timbers."

Another piece of meat. Lias swallowed it down.

"Slowly, slowly," the knight gently admonished. "So you were not born a slave, rather you were captured by traders, correct?"

"Yes."

The piece came a little more slowly this time. "Do not choke yourself."

Lias was beginning to openly weep now. He drew a shivering breath, then turned his head. "I don't want anymore, take it away!"

"That is hardly true," said the knight. "You're starving."

"I will eat no more! I will not submit to you or any other who dares call himself my master! I was a free man, not a dog on a chain! If you wish to play sick games with

17

someone, play them with the little man-whore I bit in the wagon!"

"Lias, if you trust no one, things will not get better for you."

"Grand talk from a man who chains me to a wall."

"And if I unchained you, what would you do?"

"I'd kill you and anyone else I could!"

"Then do not reprimand me for chaining you to a wall when you just proclaimed your willingness to kill me. I daresay you would do the same thing."

"I would never buy a slave to start with," growled Lias. "All I wanted was to find my wife when the traders took her! Then they took me as well! For eighteen months, all I have done is worry about her fate!"

"Was she not on the ship with you?"

Lias paused, blinking in surprise, the question causing him to consider something he had not before. *Was* she on the ship? There had been plenty of other women jammed into the hold along with the men. But... Merdine had not been among them.

"No," he said quietly, thoughtfully. "But I was sold very quickly. In less than an hour. Perhaps... I did not see her..."

"Perhaps she escaped," said the knight softly.

Or was killed. Or sold before him. Or chained up in a different ship. But no — that could not be right. The river was narrow, and the traders had to be fast. They would not use more than one ship per raid, so to be in and away as fast as possible. If they had caught Merdine, then she would have been in the ship.

Why was she not on the ship?

The knight reached out to touch him, and Lias snapped out of his reverie to lunge at that hand, biting it viciously. The knight swore and yanked it free from Lias' teeth, ripping the skin. He left without another word, taking the meat with him. Lias turned his attention once more to trying to tear his chain free, screaming and weeping as all his efforts were in vain.

18

Chapter Two

The knight left the bed chamber, ignoring the sounds of Lias raging against his chains. He gave the bowl of meat to a passing servant and walked to a large arched doorway that led outside to a wide balcony that overlooked the forests surrounding his home. The rain was coming down in torrents, and the lightning flashed across the sky, lighting up the surrounding area, showing for the briefest moment a trail of distant smoke rising from the trees.

"Not even in the rain, does it stop," muttered the knight.

He heard something shuffle behind him, and he sighed quietly as he smelled a rotted stench like every battlefield he had ever known.

"What do you want?" he asked irritably.

A tottering horror shuffled to his side, a monster made of broken bones and rotting bodies forced into some semblance of a living creature.

"Necromis, is that any way to greet your dearest friend?"

Necromis stretched, enjoying the rain. "If you were my dearest friend, then no, it would not be. Again, I ask — what do you want?"

"Only to remind you that time runs short."

"I still have a year."

"A year less three days, and this is the fifth slave you have brought home. Why do you persist in this nonsense? You were happy enough, once upon a time, in your evil. Look at all you have gained! You are a knight of the Order of the White Bear! You have a fine mansion, horses, servants, a full wine cellar... the king himself plans to name you his heir, since he has no children of his own. At least, not anymore. Why waste your time on some pointless quest for redemption?"

Necromis smiled faintly. "Perhaps I would be more content if you did not plan to kill me in one year less three days."

"That *was* the bargain. You said you would give your life to become a knight of the Order of the White Bear. To have all the things they have. Now you seek a way out of the bargain."

"Because you lied to me."

The monstrosity chuckled. "I'm a demon, it's what I do. And what lie, pray tell, great knight?"

"You said I would have *everything* they have. *Everything*. That included Sterling."

The demon sighed through its three rotting heads. "Can I help it if a master kills his slave in a fit of passion?"

"You knew the bargain included Sterling. And now he is dead when he should be here with me!"

"He belonged to another, who used him as he saw fit. Stop snivelling over a dead whore. Be grateful I gave you a chance to escape the agreement at all. Though I must say you are not having any luck. Would it amuse you to know they say I myself reside in your new little pet? It amuses *me*, certainly. I will enjoy watching you try to tame that one. He's as bitter as *you*, only far better at expressing it."

"I'll do it," said Necromis softly.

"And if you do not, there are other slaves. I will enjoy watching you lose your temper and butcher this one. He holds so much hate and anger within him that he is sure to cause you to ascend to new heights of brutality. Still, you should show him a little gratitude. He did bring you your next meal."

"Yes. I suppose he did." Necromis looked up at the night sky just as the lightning turned the dark brighter than day.

"And you will be so good as to bring the bones to my campfire in the woods," said the demon.

"Yes, yes, now be on your way. I have plans to make, and I wish to eat in peace."

The demon bowed and departed. Necromis left the balcony and the rain, heading for a locked, private chamber. He unlocked the door with a key from around his throat, then stepped inside and quietly secured the door behind himself. Within the room there were no tapestries, or rugs, or fine furnishings. There was only a stone altar, surrounded by candles, and one attendant, who looked as if someone had stitched pieces of a man and a bear together to form a ghastly puzzle. The head itself was in pieces, the right half a man, the left half a bear. The monster shuffled forward to take Necromis' robe.

"The new slave brings good fortune," said the monster. "He has saved us the trouble of a hunt tonight."

"Yes, I suppose he has, hasn't he? And no one will question what I do with my own property. I only wish I could buy my own victims. It would make these monthly sacrifices to Bonecracker so much easier. I shall bathe tonight before I dine, Ursine."

"Very good, sir."

Necromis undressed, stripping naked before walking to the center of the floor. Ursine gathered the clothing and slowly lumbered over to a sheltered alcove where the fine silks would be safe from any spray. After they were hung up, Ursine walked over to a winch and began cranking it, lowering something from the ceiling. It was the young Seven Isles slave, hanging by his ankles, and he was screaming wildly, pleading, begging, weeping for Necromis to let him go. Necromis walked over to the altar and picked up a long slender knife.

"You came here by destiny. I cannot change that," said Necromis, examining the knife. "Be content that your life shall sustain me another thirty days."

"Please let me go. I'll do anything you want me to!"

"That is a very weak offer for a slave to make! Yes, of course, you shall, and you are doing it now. Shut up and bleed."

Necromis stabbed the boy in the throat, then stood under the flow of hot blood, stroking it over his pale skin, letting it run over his white hair, licking it from his fingers. All too soon, the shower of dark crimson slowed, and Ursine lowered the still-living body so Necromis could stab his knife into the boy's belly and drag out his liver, feasting upon the bloody meat. After consuming a sizeable portion, he dropped it to the floor and tore out the heart, chewing on it as it squirted blood from its stilled chambers. When he was done feasting, he looked to Ursine.

"You may have what is left. Be sure to leave meat on the bones and wrap them. I must take them to Bonecracker."

"Yes, my lord. Thank you."

Necromis left the chamber, locking it carefully once more, walking naked across the hall to the balcony where he and Bonecracker had recently conversed, trailing blood from his long hair. As Necromis allowed the rain to clean away the worst of the blood, he thought back on his bargain with the demon.

He had done it for love. But what he had done had been so very wrong.

It had been ten years ago when he first saw Sterling. Back then, Necromis had been called Kinwill, and he had been the only son of a man who owned the livery stable in the small town where he lived. He had been tending to the feet of a fat grumpy mare when he first saw Sterling. He was pretty, with silvery hair and grey eyes, as full of mischief as a kitten and the apple of his master's eye. That had been when Kinwill had learned what a slave was. He had never known that it was possible for human beings to own other human beings. But it did not seem such a bad thing; Sterling was clearly adored and well cared for.

Kinwill often saw him in the town where he grew up, and he and Sterling became very close. His master would let Sterling come to visit, and Kinwill learned something else that summer. He learned to fall in love. One day, he went to Sterling's master and asked his cost. The man gave him a price, and Kinwill set out trying to raise it. But not all of Kinwill's methods of raising the gold were honest, and he was caught stealing from a man in a tavern. He was sent to prison, and when he emerged three years later, Sterling had a new master — one who did not let him out to play with the filthy son of a stable owner and a criminal to boot. This new master would not sell, and the few times Kinwill saw Sterling, it was clear the life was being slowly sucked out of him. He was faded and grey and sickly, and it was obvious he would not live much longer.

Kinwill could stand it no more. He went to the dark temple deep in the woods outside the village and sacrificed meat, wine, and all the gold he had earned at the temple of Bonecracker for power and wealth.

"This is not enough," said the demon. "What else will you give me?"

"My life. I give you my life!"

That seemed to satisfy it. He slew the son of a stable owner on the spot, then raised him from the dead.

"You have a new life now," Bonecracker told him. "And a new name. From this day on, Kinwill is dead, and Necromis stands in his place. Go to the edge of the forest. A house awaits you that is yours. You have eight years to remain above ground and achieve your goals. Then your bones are mine."

"And Sterling will be there?"

That was when Necromis realized that bargaining with demons had to be done carefully.

"You asked me for wealth and power. You did not ask me for your little slave boy. But perhaps you can still win him."

Necromis felt anger rise up in him. "You knew I did this for Sterling!"

"But that is not what you asked for."

Necromis had wanted to kill the monster, but there was little chance of achieving that goal. He found the house by the edge of the forest and the monstrous horrors that would serve him now. But he had no name and no station. All he had was wealth, and Sterling's master refused to sell him to a man with no standing. Necromis did what he had to in order to earn favour and recognition, but by the time he achieved them, Sterling was dead. Necromis found himself locked in a nightmare world of undeath, where once a month he had to dine on the flesh of others to sustain himself. It would have been bearable had Sterling been by his side, but he was lost in a pit of other bodies, thrown away as if he had never meant anything to anyone.

As if he had not been worth the life of one stable owner's son.

Necromis found a new goal in life: the utter destruction of the man who sold Sterling, and the man who killed him. Necromis slowly amassed power the way a tsunami amasses the waters of the sea and unleashed it with a wild vengeance, destroying each of them utterly, leaving not even their families. He took their lands, their holdings, and eventually their lives, storing them in dungeons so that he may sacrifice them at his leisure when he needed to feast. It had taken him three years to kill them all. For the following five years, he had hunted the unwary, catching them when he could, keeping them hidden, and finally killing them when need arose, all the while managing to cloak himself in an air of propriety and nobility. Not even Necromis' own servants knew what he truly was—at least, not the human ones. And the monstrous ones were kept carefully locked away and out of sight.

Over time, however, Necromis lost his taste for murder. Those who had harmed his beloved were dead, as was his beloved himself. And in the sixth year of his undead existence, he went to Bonecracker to forge a new bargain. He met with the demon by his fire before his temple in the dark woods, bringing the latest offering of bloody bones. As Bonecracker snapped them to lick the marrow, Necromis spoke what was on his mind.

"I wish to change our bargain. I know I cannot leave it, but…"

The demon licked its lips and grinned at him. "Would you *like* to leave it?"

"I would like to leave it and keep all that I have, yes."

"Then let us play a game! Or rather, a better game! You admit Sterling's death was your fault."

Necromis raised an eyebrow. "I admit at the time I was naïve as to the ways of monsters."

"Monsters, he says! Hah! And where did these fine bones you bring me come from? I may be a demon, but I do not see you shudder when the hot blood falls upon your pretty white skin. You are just as much a monster as I. That is what will make my challenge so much fun. I will release you from our bargain, if you can make a slave fall in love with you."

That sounded deceptively easy. "And that is all? Why do I find that hard to believe?"

Bonecracker grinned. "Because he cannot be just any slave. He must be angry and broken and tortured. He must be filled with hate and darkness, and *you*, my little white knight..." Bonecracker pointed a rotting finger at Necromis. "*You*, who are so full of bitterness and hate yourself, must reach into your blackened being and find the kindness needed to win him. And he cannot be a man who chooses the company of other men above a lady. That's cheating."

Necromis stared at the three-headed monstrosity as it gnawed the bleeding bones he had brought to it. "How is that cheating?"

"Makes it too easy."

That was when Necromis knew he was in very deep trouble indeed. Sterling's death had destroyed something within himself, and the subsequent murders required to sustain his undead existence had done nothing to make matters better. And to win a man not like himself? Necromis had a fleeting urge to tell the demon to simply take him to the underworld now, but it passed.

"All right. I'll play your game. How long do I have?"

"Until the eighth year of your unlife. If you have not done it by then, well..."

"Very well. I will try."

"Good! Have a bone!"

Necromis stared at the splintered femur Bonecracker offered him. "Later, perhaps."

"Come come, have a bone. The marrow is still warm in this one."

25

Bonecracker waggled the femur at him. Necromis shrugged, then accepted it along with the bargain. It was his only chance to escape his own world of darkness. But not without what he had earned. What he had given his own life for.

* * *

He washed away the worst of the blood, then descended a stone stairway from the balcony to the garden, stepping into a small, heated pool to wash himself while the rain fell and the lightning cracked. Then, once he was cleaned and his hair washed, he walked, nude, back up the stairs to the balcony and down the hall to his private chambers. He entered the room and paused, sniffing. No stink of urine this time. He cast a glance to Lias and found him sitting on his small bed, staring hate at his master. Necromis smiled faintly.

"If you were this beautiful, you would not bother with clothes either."

Lias rolled his eyes. Well, at least that was an emotion other than blind hate. Necromis locked his bedroom door, then walked to a wardrobe to get himself a nightshirt. After he dressed in the simple garment of white cotton, he seated himself before a mirror to brush out his long white hair.

"Let us play a game, you and I. One that does not involve you spitting, biting, or pissing."

Lias stared at him, his expression telling Necromis that he had little interest in any games. Necromis began braiding his long damp hair back. In the morning, it would be dry and wavy, forming an elegant mane. As he braided, he spoke to Lias.

"It's called the 'Let's Make Friends' game. Do you wish to play?"

An empty tin water pitcher flew by, narrowly missing Necromis' head. Necromis paid it absolutely no mind as he preened.

"I am assuming that is a 'no.'"

"Let me go!"

26

Necromis finished the single long braid in his white hair and bound it with a ribbon. "Lias, you bit my hand, pissed on my tapestry — on my heraldic crest, no less — and threatened to kill me. What sort of fool would I be to let you off that chain?"

Necromis heard Lias pick up a second metal object. Without looking, he pointed a finger at him.

"Lias, if you hurl that chamber pot, I swear to all that is dark within myself that I will skin you alive and bathe you in salt."

The pot was set aside. Good. The fool did have *some* modicum of self-preservation after all. Necromis picked up a bottle of very costly scent and began dabbing it on himself.

"You're awfully pretty for a man," said Lias. Necromis could tell that Lias did not mean it as a compliment.

"I broke the lower jaw off a demon-drake in battle with my bare hands," said Necromis. "If I marched to war in a full ball gown and glass slippers with bows in my hair, grown warriors would still shit in their armor at the sight of me. One does not become a knight of the Order of the White Bear without certain abilities. Therefore, I can be as pretty as I damn please. And you're just jealous."

"Of what?" Lias sounded genuinely surprised.

"That you're not pretty."

"I'm no woman!"

Necromis looked to the man on the small bed. His black hair was wild, and his eyes were almost liquid blue. He was strong from years of felling trees and hauling lumber, and even after all the beatings and torture and starvation, Necromis could tell this was a very attractive man. All he needed was some feeding and healing. He smiled faintly.

"No, you certainly are not. You are definitely a man."

Lias stared at Necromis sourly. "You touch me, and I swear that, while you may violate my body, you will not be pretty by the end of it."

27

"Lias, I have no intention of forcing myself on you. None. Not because I don't think you are lovely, but because it is wrong. What joy is there in using an act that is supposed to be of love and bonding to inflict hurt, hate, and humiliation? I would not do that to you. The only way I would have you in my bed is willingly."

"That will *never* happen."

Necromis glanced to an ornate gold and porcelain clock, noting it was past midnight. *Well, I have a year less four days now to persuade you otherwise.*

"Are you hungry?" asked Necromis.

"I will never eat again."

"I did not ask you if you intended to eat. I asked if you were hungry."

"What does it matter if I have no intention of eating?"

Necromis picked up a pair of metal gauntlets and put them on as Lias watched. "Because you're going to eat whether you like it or not."

Necromis picked up a covered dish and lifted the lid, setting it aside. There was a very small pile of strange-looking, greyish-black moss; a type of lichen that grew on certain rotted logs deep within the darkest swamps. It was known for its powerful sedative effects. A tiny amount would sweeten Lias' vicious disposition, at least long enough to get dinner into him. Holding a few small sprigs of the moss in his fingers, Necromis turned to Lias and smiled.

"Open wide."

Lias raged against his chain, spitting, biting, swearing, thrashing. At one point, he almost managed to subdue Necromis with the chain, but the powerful knight freed himself. Using his own weight, he forced Lias to the floor and shoved the moss down his throat, his fingers well protected from Lias' teeth by the gauntlets. All that was left for Necromis to do then was pull back and watch the moss take effect. Lias choked and coughed, staring at Necromis.

"I will kill you. This I swear on the grave of my wife Elyssa. I will see you dead by my hand."

28

"Someday, perhaps," said Necromis softly.

He watched as Lias snarled and raged, gradually weakening, becoming slower, soon hardly able to hold up his own head. Necromis removed his gantlets and walked over to Lias, moving him from the stone floor and onto his bed. Necromis seated himself on the bed as well, Lias' head in his lap. He smiled, toying with the black hair.

"There now, this is much nicer."

Lias blinked, blue eyes following the paths of invisible creatures. "You do mean to rape me."

"No, I intend to do something far more cruel. I intend to comb this hair of yours." Necromis reached up to pull the ornate ribbon of fabric attached to a bell, summoning a servant.

"What are these creatures I am seeing?" asked Lias. "Rabbits and birds..."

Necromis drew out a comb and began gently picking at the formidable knots in Lias' hair. "Tell me about them."

"I see rabbits," said Lias in a near-whisper. "They are dancing in a field of wildflowers, and there is sunlight. I see trees, and birds, and clear water in a pond... what magic is this?"

"It is no magic," said Necromis gently. "It is a natural effect of the herb. It soothes the heart and shows us things that please us. Any sight you wish to see, it will show it to you."

Lias' eyes watched unseen wonders. "I see my daughters dancing in the meadow with the rabbits. I see a great grey wolf, but he means no harm, he has come only to drink cream from a pail. Little Sunni is riding him like a pony. She is my youngest. Why are you pulling my hair?"

"I am attempting to comb it, but never has a knight been thus defeated before."

"The ghost of my first wife will show up to tell you that you are wasting your time."

Necromis smiled faintly. "You loved her."

29

"She was my world, a true lady, well above me in station. Why she graced me with her love and gave me children, I do not know. I was unworthy of her."

"Clearly, she did not think so," said Necromis.

Lias struggled briefly, as if trying to escape, but ultimately collapsing once more. "Don't speak of her, you bastard. You show me all this to weaken me, to force me to feel some friendship for you. I do not know why you wish for me to call you friend, but it will not happen. I will not give in to your freakish whims."

Necromis felt a violent rage well up inside himself, and, in that instant, he nearly killed Lias. But something held him back. Some voice of reason, almost lost to him these days, told him that Lias was his final hope. He could not keep killing off his slaves out of anger, then wasting time seeking a suitable replacement. Lias *was* his last chance — he was angry, bitter, despondent, and favoured women. Necromis had to stand his ground against his demonic tendencies if he wished to end this curse.

"What is so freakish about wishing to have your friendship?" asked Necromis, still carefully picking at the black hair despite his urge to tear it out at the roots.

"No man buys another man and forces him to feel companionship for no reason."

"You are right," said Necromis. "I am lonely. A slave cannot betray you."

"I do not believe you. I believe no one anymore. I have been dragged from my home and sold like meat time and time again. Men have forced themselves on me, chained me, flogged me, and one even put me in a walled yard from which I could not escape in order to better teach his son to use a bow on a moving target. I will hate you until I die."

"Or I do," said Necromis softly.

If Lias heard the remark, he gave no indication. Necromis continued to comb the wild and matted black hair until a servant arrived. Merrigale set down the tray of food she was carrying, then turned to face her master, hands on her rather broad hips.

"My lord, what *are* you doing?"

"Combing my slave's hair and failing rather miserably at the task."

"Some sweet-oil will ease out the tangles. Have you tried it?"

Necromis examined a particularly wicked knot. "Actually, I'm wondering if it would not be easier to simply shave the whole thing off."

She rolled her eyes. "Have you any tasks for me?"

"No, thank you. I'm just going to comb out these knots and then try to feed him before the herbs wear off."

"Master, may I speak?"

Necromis pulled something live and wiggling out of Lias' hair and held it up, studying it. "I've certainly never been able to stop you in the past."

She brought him the glass bottle of sweet-oil. "Master... I know you have never spoken to me of the slaves you have brought home, nor is it any of my affair, but... but time and again, I see you buy the worst of the worst and then try to win their friendship for reasons that are very much your own. But each time... I see you make the same mistakes."

"Mistakes? Don't be ridiculous, I am a knight of the Order of the White Bear. I'm perfect." Necromis watched sourly as the stopper on the top of the bottle popped off and dumped the costly contents all over Lias' head. "Save for when I am accidentally spilling too much oil all over my slave."

Merrigale fetched him a towel. "I know not why it is important to you to win their friendship, but there can be no friendship without trust. How can he trust you when you drug him and then discuss shaving his head?"

"Well, if I do not, he bites!"

"Of course, he bites. He's probably terrified!" The matronly woman sat down on the floor beside the low bed and helped to dab up the spilled oil. "You must show him he has nothing to fear. Show him what a good and kind knight I know you to be, what all your servants know you to be!

31

That you would never hurt a soul without just cause or to defend your king."

Or to buy myself another thirty days of life, thought Necromis. "Merrigale... I am really not certain I know how to do that. And that has been the whole problem. This is important to me. I cannot explain to you, why, or how much..."

"We all *know* why," said Merrigale. "It's because of the slave boy you loved."

Necromis sighed, berating himself for not realizing how astute his own staff could be. Of course, it was hardly a secret he loved Sterling. That he hid from no one. The part he did hide was the bargain he made with Bonecracker. *That* he had carefully ensured no one knew. He could not remain a knight if that bit of news reached the king.

"It... is because of him," said Necromis, continuing to comb out Lias' hair.

"We will help if we are able," said Merrigale. "He has no reason to fear you."

"I'm not so sure about that," said Necromis, examining Lias' hair. It had gone from a web of tangles to a collection of random spikes. He tried to comb it down and found it became worse. He sighed loudly. "Well, he's never going to forgive *this* mess."

Merrigale took the comb and tried her hand at the chaos of mats. After a few minutes, she shook her head. "It's just too thick. Well, there is nothing for it now. We will just have to wait for the oil to dry."

Necromis rubbed the towel over Lias' head in an attempt to remove most of the oil. When he was done, the heavy black hair stood up like the fur on an angry cat's back.

"I concede defeat," said Necromis.

"There is wisdom in your decision," said Merrigale. "Well, I have brought you your sliced fruit and cold water with lemon. Have you need of anything else?"

"No, Merrigale, thank you. Good night."

"Good night, my lord." Merrigale departed.

Necromis looked down at Lias. "So did any of that conversation reach you?"

Lias blinked sleepily, watching something only he could see.

"Apparently not," Necromis grumbled.

He was able to feed the fruit to Lias, then left him on the bed to sleep. Necromis had no doubt that Lias would hate him just as much in the morning, but there was little he could do about that, save take Merrigale's advice and try to win Lias' trust.

How could a man with so many secrets win the trust of anyone?

Chapter Three

Necromis awoke early. A glance across the room from his own bed to the small one near the wall showed Lias was still deep in sleep, his black hair a wild tangle. Apparently, that was simply his hair's natural state.

Necromis pushed the blankets back and sat up, stretching. He then unbraided his long hair, shaking it out before oiling and combing it so that it shone like mercury. He chose his clothing carefully, something that left little doubt as to his status as a knight. Since he was to inherit the throne when the king died, assuming he did not die first, he was obligated to appear at the castle twice a week to learn his duties. Necromis did not especially wish to become king, but he could hardly decline the offer when it was made. For one thing, it would have been a slap in the face to a king who loved him, and for another, he could think of several others who would look upon the title as a chance to do little more than carry on like drunken bandits.

He dressed in a tunic and breeches, then drew on a chainmail shirt. Over that, he wore a second tunic, the collar and sleeves trimmed in white bear fur, the symbol of the white bear, rampant on a red field, emblazoned on the front. He drew on his boots, then his long white cloak. Ensuring his hair flowed free down his back, he dabbed on some scent, then checked himself in the mirror. He always looked his finest after a blood bath, and today was no exception. His skin was white as milk, and his eyes almost luminously green. Perhaps a little kohl around the eyes would bring out...

"You preen like a woman."

Oh, jolly joy, somebody was awake.

"No," said Necromis. "Women preen like me. But if they are half as pretty as I, then no wonder. Did you sleep well?"

"I dreamed I killed you then pissed in your skull."

"So an enjoyable night's sleep. Well, you will have to keep your charm to yourself for today. I have places to go. But never fear, dear Lias, I shall be back."

"I hope your horse falls and snaps his neck and lands on top of you."

"Really, Lias, that's hardly nice. What did my horse ever do to you?" Necromis carefully lined his eyes in kohl, then touched his pale lips with just a hint of colour with some cosmetics in a small pot. He applied a tiny amount to his cheeks as well, then stood back and admired himself.

"Ah, Necromis, you shame the world with your beauty." He looked to Lias. "What do you think?"

"Are you a knight or a whore?"

"Well now, that depends entirely on the company and the amount of drink. Of course, after I am king, I will have to select one man to stand beside me as Royal Consort."

"King?"

For once, Lias sounded surprised as opposed to hostile. Necromis paused in his preening to look at him. The man's blue eyes were large, the expression... almost hopeful.

"Yes, king. As you know, the king of our fair land lost all of his children in our last war with the island nation of Gablesen. Since I am his favourite knight, he has decided to declare me heir."

Necromis preened. Lias sat up, his eyes definitely more hopeful.

"Did you mean it when you said you wished to be my friend?"

"Yes," said Necromis. "I did. Why?"

"A man as powerful as you should be able to find a handful of filthy traders and make them tell you what they did with my wife."

Necromis tossed his head, watching his hair shimmer. "Yes, I suppose I could. But I *will* want something in return. I do not demand that you love me, but I *do* demand that you respect me. Agreed? I do not rescue fair maids for louts."

35

Lias nodded. "I agree," he said quietly.

"Very well. Here. Take these." Necromis gave Lias a pen, jar of ink, and some paper. "Write down everything you recall about the night she was taken. We will discuss it when I return. I cannot leave the king waiting."

"Wait! I cannot write! Nor can I read!"

"Then I will send up a servant to attend you. Now I really must be gone, Lias."

Necromis left the room in a flurry of white fur, hastily buckling his sword belt about his waist. As he was going down the stairs, he saw Merrigale coming up.

"Your horse is saddled," she called.

"Thank you, Merrigale, you are a blessing. Oh! Send a servant who is able to read and write to attend Lias, would you please?"

"I hardly think he has anything to say worth recording," she remarked.

Necromis would have liked to have responded, but his appointment with the king was a little too pressing for banter. He left his house and went down the white stone steps to the gravel carriageway before his house. His horse was a huge white beast, with a black muzzle, four black stockings, and a black mane and tail. Necromis approached the gigantic animal and took the reins, kissing the soft nose.

"Hello, Rufus. How are you this fine morning?"

"My lord, honestly," said the groom. "It is a black and white horse. Why call him Rufus?"

"He looks like a Rufus." Necromis took hold of the saddle, put his foot into the stirrup, and swung himself up. The ground was indeed very far away when seated on Rufus. He was a true giant of an animal, bred not to carry knights into battle but to haul lumber and heavy timbers for ships. He was docile, with a noble demeanor, and large enough to crush the skull of another knight's horse with one blow from his burnished hoof. Necromis loved the animal.

"He looks like the business end of some giant's mop gone for a run," said the groom.

Necromis ignored him and turned Rufus to the road. The immense animal pranced along, tail, mane, and leg feathers all flying and flapping. Necromis stroked the horse's neck.

"Pay no mind to him, Rufus," said Necromis. "When we get home, I'll let you shit on his herb garden. I'm sure he will appreciate your generous gift of fertilizer."

Rufus snorted, bobbing his head as he cantered along the road, enjoying being out in the sun. He did not need to be told where to go; he had been along this road often enough. Necromis could use the time to read over his notes from the last lessons, while Rufus pranced and bobbed his head, shaking his long mane.

It was nearly an hour before Necromis saw the castle loom into view. It was a truly enormous structure, cut of red and white stone, surrounded by a formidable wall of razorstone. It was utterly black rock and prone to shatter, but that was what made it such a terrifying defense. Any hard blow from enemy ballista would see a lethal rain of deadly shards of razor-sharp rocks falling down upon the attackers, slicing flesh and armor alike to the bone.

Few would dare attack the great red and white castle of Ixander's king.

Necromis rode up the road to the great gate, which was opened at this hour of the day. He entered the village that resided within the safety of the walls. He was greeted by an old man with a skewer of meat, grinning. Necromis tossed him a coin and accepted the meat as he rode by.

"Aldus, you are a mind reader!" called Necromis from over his shoulder.

"Nay, I just have a good ear for horse hooves! I can tell your big fellow from a mile away!"

Necromis laughed and devoured the meat as he crossed the last few meters to the castle. He dismounted before the great structure, allowing a groom to take his horse, and ascended the wide, scarlet stairs. He entered the huge structure and made his way to the Morning Room, where the king and his favoured knights would be gathered.

The king was not there when Necromis arrived, but his retinue of favourites were.

"There's my pretty boy!" shouted Blassard from across the room.

Necromis smiled, removing his cloak as the hairy mountain of a man swooped in to hug him. Necromis detected the unmistakable smell of strong drink and far too much of it. That was odd. Blassard was not a man given to early morning drunkenness. Necromis endured his customary embrace.

"Good morning, Blassard," said Necromis.

"Good morning, good morning!" the man greeted him, hugging him enthusiastically, much to the amusement of the others in the room.

Necromis made a face as Blassard kissed his cheek, then pressed a mug of ale into his hands. "Blassard, are you drunk?"

"No, no, just merry, is all. Come sit on Uncle's knee." Blassard seated himself clumsily on a chair, pulling Necromis onto his lap, much to the hilarity of those gathered.

Necromis turned his head to glare at the much older knight. "Blassard…"

"Do you want Uncle to tell you a story?"

"Yes, tell me the one about the knight who showed up drunk to breakfast."

Blassard laughed. "Later, later. Have you met Sir Barton?"

Necromis looked in the direction Blassard indicated and found himself gazing at an unfamiliar face. Necromis thought he detected a reason for Blassard's uncharacteristic behaviour; both wore the insignia of the Order of the Boar. Quite likely, Blassard feared being replaced as a Favourite, and at his age, that would be a devastating blow indeed. However, as the heir to the throne, Necromis would never let that happen. He was far too fond of Blassard and considerably less fond of upstarts. Necromis struggled to his feet, helped along by a hearty swat on the bottom from Blassard. Necromis turned on him.

"Sir Blassard, would you mind humiliating me in your customary manner — in private?"

"Very sorry," said Blassard, trying not to smile. "I'll behave."

Necromis doubted that, but he turned to Sir Barton, setting aside his mug of ale. "So we have a second member of the Order of the Boar in our midst. To what do we owe the pleasure?"

Sir Barton was ugly, hairy, and slovenly. It was hardly the first time Necromis had met a knight with any one of those qualities, but rarely did he encounter one with all three. This pig could not possibly be a Favourite. Nothing that stunk could hold such a position, and he did indeed smell. Sir Barton wiped his hands on his tunic and continued to chew and breathe through his mouth as he spoke.

"Sir Blassard spoke so highly of you, I wished to see the great Necromis of the Bear for myself. My. You certainly are... pretty."

"Meaning?"

"Oh, nothing. Only that I had not expected a man who allegedly can break the jaw of a demon-drake with his bare hands to be so fair."

Sir Hawthorne rose to his feet. He was tall, with hair the colour of gold, blue eyes, and a scar across his left cheek from the paw of a great cat. He was strong and handsome. Necromis had long had an eye for him, but Sir Hawthorne did not return the feeling. He did, however, return the respect.

"I would not bait Sir Necromis, if I were you. Pretty as he may be, he has *earned* his place in the order."

Another knight spoke up — Sir Thordin. "And *some* people would do well to copy his sense of dress and cleanliness."

There were chuckles. Necromis smiled. This man was winning no friends. If Sir Barton thought insulting Necromis would make him popular, he was quickly learning

39

that he was wrong. Sir Barton seemed to think this was not going as anticipated. He looked rather uncomfortable and shifted nervously on his feet.

"Your pardon, Sir," he said meekly.

"I do not grant pardon to filthy brats who think it is appropriate to stand in the Room of the Favourites wearing three banquets' worth of food and casting insult upon his betters," said Necromis.

Sir Barton was clearly showing signs of embarrassment. "I meant only…"

Necromis narrowed his green eyes. "You meant only to make sport of me in hopes of winning yourself a place among us. What you fail to understand is not one of us came to be here through wit or dress or fawning. We came here because we are the strongest knights in the realm. Not the foulest."

"I have fought in battle," said Sir Barton.

"Wrestling with a joint of pork does not count," snarled Necromis.

Sir Barton found his spine. "It was in the Grey Fields! I fought there!"

"As did I," said Necromis. "I do not recall the name of Sir Barton."

"I was not a knight then, so that is hardly surprising."

Necromis raised an eyebrow. "You're hardly a knight now. Begone from my sight. You're not one of us. You have no place here."

Sir Barton departed. Necromis allowed himself to be pulled onto Blassard's lap once more.

"Tell me you were not worried about that stinking heap claiming your chair here in this room," said Necromis.

"Nay, nay," said Blassard. "I only brought him because he whined so often about meeting you. The meeting went exactly as I knew it would. He is a good knight but given to fancies. He sees a man who takes pleasure in his own beauty and assumes him to be weak. He made the same mistake about Lady Solecil over there."

40

Lady Solecil was drinking from a mug with her left hand, her right being gone from the elbow. Her right eye, too, was gone. She had fought on the Grey Fields as well and lost her arm and eye to the dead things that slithered out of the ground in the evening fog, freezing anything they touched. Many had lost limbs and more.

"His presence here was unwelcome and fetid," said Solecil.

"Why bring him at all?" asked Necromis.

"He's young," said Blassard dismissively. "He needs his lessons yet. He thinks one great battle makes him a hero and grants him airs."

"It does not grant him the right to stand here and challenge Necromis," said Hawthorne. "A knight of less even temper would have slain him for such insult."

Necromis feigned a swoon. "Compliments from my beloved! Could it be today shall be the day we run away together?"

"Nay," said Hawthorne with mock gravity. "I discussed it with my wife. She said if I run off with you, then she shall be close behind all the days of my life, which she assures me shall be brief and painful."

"Shameful," said Necromis. "We shall settle for breakfast then. Where is His Majesty this fine morning?"

"His Royal Highness is unwell," said Hawthorne.

"Not serious, I hope," said Necromis.

"Nay, not serious," said Hawthorne softly. "But he is rather aged. Days such as these are to be expected. We will stay until our usual time, then depart. Did I hear you purchased a new slave?"

"I did," said Necromis, paying no heed to Blassard as he fell asleep, mouth open, snoring.

"Honestly, Necromis," said Solecil, her tone gentle. "It's time to move on."

"I cannot yet," said Necromis. "In time, I will, but not yet."

41

"But why, Necromis?" asked Thordin. "Why bring home these angry, bitter slaves who are of no use to anyone?"

Necromis lowered his head, his long hair falling over his face as he gazed into his ale. He slowly drew a steadying breath, then spoke. "Sterling told me that everyone can be redeemed. I need to believe that."

There was a long, solemn silence as the knights pondered the words of the dead slave Necromis had loved. Then the silence was interrupted by a noise not unlike some great air-filled bladder slowly leaking. The sound rose in volume and intensity, accompanied by a stench as if something had escaped the bowels of an undead cow. Necromis set aside his ale and looked over his shoulder at Blassard as he snored in his drunken slumber.

"And thus, my dear friend has proven my beloved wrong, for *nothing* can redeem that which hath passed."

"Let us have breakfast in the music room," said Lady Solecil. "I do not wish to eat anything which has been in contact with this air! Augh! Run! He's doing it again! Oh, gods, I feel faint!" Solecil pretended to be on the verge of fainting.

Thordin rose to his feet. "I shall save you, fair maiden!"

"I, too, feel faint!" said Necromis.

"Farewell, good Necromis, I shall think fondly of your memory."

Necromis rose to his feet and followed his companions out of the room. "Thordin, it has only just now occurred to me that you are a bastard."

The knights left the room, but as they did so, Necromis took hold of Hawthorne's sleeve and drew him aside, looking into his friend's eyes.

"You and I both know Blassard to be too good a knight to show up drunk to the king's breakfast table. What is wrong?"

Hawthorne sighed quietly, clearly unwilling to speak of the matter. Eventually, however, he did.

42

"The chirurgeon has examined him and found his heart and lungs to be failing. I am sorry, Necromis. I know how very fond you are of Blassard, but his time in the battle of Grey Fields and then the months spent working there afterwards with the holy men to clear away the evil for good has cost him gravely. It is late spring now. He will not see winter."

Necromis' legs failed him, and he sat down hard on the floor. Hawthorne sat beside him, taking hold of Necromis' hand and looking into his eyes, clearly concerned for his friend.

"Necromis?"

Necromis felt his body begin to shake, and Hawthorne's voice seemed to come from very far away. His heart beat strangely in his chest, and it seemed as if he would die where he sat. Blassard had been his dearest friend for as long as Necromis had existed as Necromis. His loss was more than tragic and heartbreaking; it was like some fell omen, warning of his own failure to meet Bonecracker's conditions.

At any other time, Necromis would have done his best to wring every drop of pleasure out of being close to Hawthorne, but as the tall man picked him up from the floor, Necromis was barely aware of his presence. Blassard was dying. It was as if all the hope and joy in life was being sucked from his very flesh. It was several minutes before he realized he had been moved to a daybed in a private room, and Hawthorne was seated beside him, holding his hand and gazing down at him.

"Did I faint?" asked Necromis.

"Very nearly," said Hawthorne. "I admit, I knew you would take the news hard, but..."

"Is there no way to save him?"

"Not without a journey into the woods to the Endless Fire before the temple of Bonecracker," said Hawthorne. "And we all know how such bargains end."

"Yes," whispered Necromis. He knew far too well how such bargains end.

43

"I'm very sorry, Necromis."

"He's the only family I have," said Necromis. "He's taught me so much. I know we are not bound by blood, but he is more my uncle than some who are."

"Why don't you ride home?" said Hawthorne softly. "I was to be your instructor for today, so we will move your lesson to after dinner, when you have had some time to rest."

"Then I insist you join me at my table this eve," said Necromis. "My cook is serving swan's eggs and roast boar."

"That is a great deal of food for just you," said Hawthorne.

"Well, it is a young boar."

Hawthorne laughed quietly. "I will be there."

Necromis gazed at him, green eyes blinking sleepily. "It's a shame."

"What is?" asked Hawthorne.

"I once said to Blassard that I could think of nothing that would overshadow my desire for you, but this has done it. The thought of his loss has darkened my want to a mere listless shadow."

"I am most sorry to hear this," said Hawthorne. "Here is a little gift to raise your spirits."

Hawthorne leaned forward and gave him a soft, brief kiss; a warm pressing of lips that, under other circumstances, would have set Necromis' flesh on fire with want. But even his passion was cold and in the ground this day. He touched Hawthorne's face gently, then slowly sat up. He felt as if the life was draining out of him.

"I will ride home," said Necromis. "Dinner will be at twilight time. I do not know how long we shall be at our lessons, so I invite you in advance to spend the night."

"Thank you, Necromis. I will be there."

Necromis smiled at him, then left the castle to claim his horse and ride home.

Chapter Four

Lias watched Necromis flit out of the room, idly wondering how anything that big could *flit*. He then looked down at the paper he held, carefully examining it. Real paper. He'd never met anyone who could afford real paper, much less freely hand it to a slave. Carefully, Lias set the sheets aside and the pen and ink as well. If Necromis was really going to help him find his wife, then he had best not be destroying valuable items such as these.

Merrigale came into the room, bearing a bowl of hot porridge for him, with honey and cream in it.

"This cannot be for me," he said as she gave it to him.

"No, it is for the slave seated beside you," she said dryly. "Sir Necromis says you are to be attended by a servant who can read and write."

"Yes," said Lias. "He promised to help me find my wife. He wished for me to put my memories of that night on paper, and he would help me to find her."

"Necromis is a very kind man," she said, gathering up the pen, ink, and paper, which were of no use to Lias. "You will learn that in time."

"Then what is my purpose? Why buy a slave? And why buy one in my state? I'm nothing more than bones, scars, and hate."

"He loved a slave once," said Merrigale, tidying the room as Lias ate.

"And he ran away?"

"Hush, you. He did not run away. He was murdered by his owner, who would not sell him to Necromis. Since then, the Master has a strange compulsion to buy slaves, make them well, and release them. You are not the first."

"Really? May I speak with one of them?"

"They are not here," said Merrigale.

Oh, that sounded rather suspicious. "Then where are they?" Lias inquired as Merrigale fluffed pillows and straightened sheets.

"At the Master's hunting lodge in the Great Forest. It requires maintaining as he does not live there all year."

Well, that could be possible. A knight as wealthy as Necromis would likely need quite a few servants, and not all of them would live here in this one manor.

"Have you ever been to the lodge, Merrigale?"

"Hah! I've enough to do here. Let others clean the kennels."

"But you have no reason to think those slaves are not at the hunting lodge?"

"No, of course, not," said Merrigale, bustling quickly about the room as she tidied. "I have worked here seven years, and never once have I seen the Master raise a hand to any who did not bring it on themselves. He is good and kind and fair, and if he says the slaves are at the lodge, I've no reason to doubt him. Now let me see about finding you someone to help you with your list."

She left the room, moving quickly. Lias sighed and lay down on his bed, musing on what he had learned. So Sir Necromis lost a slave he loved due to the cruelty of another, and now he sought out slaves to help. Seemed perfectly logical.

So why did Lias not believe it?

The door opened, and a young woman peered into the room, not much more than a girl. Her eyes were almost freakishly large, as if some deity tried to make her cute and failed utterly. Her hair was long and brown, tied up with a pink ribbon. Her dress was pink also, and the long white apron and pink-striped stockings that peeked out just above her shoes told Lias her duties were likely in the nursery.

Why would a knight, who preferred to bed other men, have a nurse on duty? It seemed unlikely to Lias that any of his lovers would have borne him a child. Perhaps Necromis had taken in a child? He did seem to have a habit of bringing home stray slaves. Perhaps he brought home

46

stray infants as well. But Lias could not see any of those infants sleeping quietly with *this* nurse in the room. She was abnormally thin, and her over-all appearance was like that of a badly made doll. A kind man with little skill crafted wood into what was meant to be a child's toy and created a nightmare. She walked over to the bed and seated herself daintily on the floor.

"Hello. You're Lias, aren't you?"

"Yes," he said warily, catching a very faint whiff of something unpleasant. As if she had been working with meat turned foul.

"I'm Nurse Bonnifas. Nice to meet you."

"Does Necromis have children?" Lias asked, not liking this strange woman.

"No," she said. "Though he beds men like he thinks it's only a matter of trying hard enough. It is tradition to have a nurse and a nursery. So here I am. I have the finest job in all the land: I tend invisible babies."

She tittered at her own joke. Her breath smelled as if she had been eating the spoiled meat as well as working with it. Lias carefully withdrew as far as he could, not wanting to hurt her feelings but not wishing to smell her either. She reached into a pocket of her apron and drew out a small pad of paper scraps. It looked like something she had made herself out of remnants she had found over time. She then withdrew a little vial of ink and a pen.

"So what is it the master wished you to say?"

"He wanted me to tell him of the night my wife was taken."

"Oh! Yes, I can see how he would enjoy hearing about that."

Lias eyed the strange nurse. "No, he said he was going to help me find her."

"Is that what he told you?" She tittered again. "Oh, goodness, he and that old bitch Merrigale certainly do tell some tall tales."

Lias did not like the direction this conversation was taking. "What are you talking about?"

47

She giggled and rolled her freakishly large eyes. "Let me guess. You're a slave, you've been mistreated, Necromis desperately wishes to earn your love and friendship, and to do that, he will help you find your missing beloved wife. Am I right?"

Lias felt the rage within himself stir like a waking dragon. "Yes. What is so funny?"

"Nothing, I assure you, nothing about this is funny. I simply must laugh or go mad with the horror of it. Lias, do not waste your time in false hope. He will not help you find your wife. He will tempt you with dreams and fantasies until you permit him to lay with you then he will sacrifice you to Bonecracker."

Lias rolled his eyes. "He is a knight of the Order of the White Bear. Lure me into his bed, I can see him trying, but no knight of that order prays to Bonecracker."

"Are you quite certain?" asked Bonnifas.

"Quite," said Lias firmly.

Bonnifas leaned forward, her breath like some warm oozing serpent looking to crush the life from him. "Do you not know where we sit? This house rests at the very edge of Blackwood. Bonecracker's eternal fire that burns before his temple can be seen from the windows. Why would a knight of the Order of the White Bear tolerate something so dark so close at hand? Would he not, at the very least, move his household? Why stay so close to that dark temple? What did Merrigale tell you about the five slaves before you? That they had gone off to some magical hunting lodge to work there? The master has no hunting lodge, Lias. Those slaves are gutted and dead, and their bones sent to the fire in the woods and the monster who warms himself beside it."

"I do not believe you," said Lias, but even as he spoke the words, he was not so certain he did not. After all the cruelty he had suffered, it seemed more likely to him than the story of lost love and redemption.

"Don't you?" whispered Bonnifas. "Then where did I get this pretty gift from?"

48

She reached into a hidden pocket beneath her apron and drew something out wrapped in white cloth. She drew aside the fabric, and Lias stared at the small white hand, severed just above the wrist—a hand that bore unmistakable marks of his own teeth.

Lias screamed, jumping to his feet. Bonnifas fled the room, giggling, as Lias began raging at his chain, desperate now to escape. He pulled and clawed at the iron plate holding the chain in place until his fingers bled and were so torn and injured, the pain forced him to stop. He then tried to push the collar over his head until the skin around his throat and jaw were torn, and the blood ran down the chain. Frantic with terror and yet another betrayal, he kept trying to escape until the door opened and Necromis appeared. Without thinking, Lias snatched up the chamber pot and hurled it at the knight, covering him liberally in filth and cutting his face.

Lias recalled little after that; only that somehow Necromis suddenly had a whip and he used it, flogging Lias as if he had gone mad with rage. The beating seemed to go on forever until some servants arrived and stopped it, dragging Necromis away. Lias lay on his bed, bleeding and torn and more dead than alive. He had not been strong when Necromis purchased him; the whipping was very nearly more than his already battered body could take.

Lias lay on his bed and closed his eyes, waiting to die.

* * *

When Lias was next aware of anything, it was dark, and someone was gently cleaning his injuries. There were people in the room, and Lias could hear them speaking.

"Master, had I not seen that display with my own eyes, I would have never thought you capable of such things."

"Ordinarily, I am not, Merrigale," said Necromis softly. "But bad news and a full chamber pot do not tend to make one feel merry. Hawthorne, how is he?"

Lias heard the man tending him, presumably Hawthorne, speak. "Bad. Very bad. His condition was deplorable to begin with. If he survives the night... well, he may, but I find it unlikely."

"Why would he attack you?" asked Merrigale.

"I do not know," said Necromis. "I was speaking to him just this morning. He asked me to help him find his wife. I asked him to make a list, and he said he could not read, nor could he write. I asked you to send a slave to tend him. Merrigale, who did you send?"

"I sent no one. We have only two servants on staff who can read and write. Both were down in the storeroom, taking inventory of the household provisions. I was going to send one of them up to speak with Lias when they were done."

"Well, something set him off," said Necromis. "Unless he is mad, there is no reason he should rapidly turn from being civil to raging like a wild thing and hurling shit."

"We will have to ask him," said Merrigale.

"Well, if any can mend him, it will be Hawthorne," said Necromis. "After all, he fixed my face. Will it scar, do you think?"

"Perhaps a little. I would not concern myself if I were you," said Merrigale.

Lias opened his eyes, unable to resist checking out what he had done to Necromis' pretty face. The pot's edge must have struck perfectly. The cut went across his cheek in a curved line that could not be anything other than a chamber pot. He would not be passing *that* mark off to his friends as a battle scar. The man tending to him seemed surprised that Lias had opened his eyes.

"Well, look who is awake," he said.

Necromis stepped closer. "Ask him why he attacked me."

Before Hawthorne could, Lias responded, his voice weak, a bare whisper. "Tell the murdering bastard I saw the severed hand of the Seven Isles slave. Tell him I know he

50

pays tithe in blood and bone to the thing that lives in the woods."

Only Lias saw the look of utter horror and fear on Necromis' face. Merrigale and Hawthorne were too busy staring at Lias to notice. In that moment, Lias knew that at least part of what the strange nurse said was true.

"Who showed you such a thing!" demanded Merrigale.

"The nursemaid, Bonnifas. She had it in her apron."

"Nursemaid?" exclaimed Hawthorne. "I assure you that Necromis has no nursemaid and is unlikely ever to need one."

"There is no nursemaid here!" confirmed Merrigale.

"So the slave is lying," said Lias bitterly. "Ask your darling master about the five slaves before me. Ask him why he endures the nearness of Bonecracker's fire!"

Hawthorne sighed loudly. "We *all* endure that fire. It moves throughout these woods, as does the temple it burns before and the beast that dwells within it. If we could catch it, we could put an end to it, but nothing with a good and decent heart can reach that flame. Only those filled with hate and anger can find it. I'd wager it burns there for you before I thought it burned for Necromis."

"That still does not explain why a nursemaid who reeks of rotted meat has a severed hand in her apron pocket. The hand of a Seven Isles slave that I bit! And if she does not live here, then how did she know to come to this room with paper and pen?"

"We will solve this mystery," said Hawthorne. "You sleep."

Lias was forced to drink down a white potion in a vial that tasted oddly of honey and pine needles. Then the world went dark.

* * *

When Lias next awoke, the sun was up, and he could hear birds singing quietly in the trees. The windows in the grand bedchamber were open, and there was a soft perfume of trees, flowers, and herbs filling the air. Lias

51

found he could not move. Not because he was tied down on any way, but because he was in so much agony that he dared not. His entire body burned and ached, and he wished he had died in the night. He noted bitterly that he was not chained, nor was he attended. Clearly, no one believed he was going anywhere.

The door opened, and in walked the knight Necromis had called Hawthorne. He had a scroll in his hands and was reading it. Lias watched him, in too much pain to move, nearly too much to breathe. Hawthorne finished reading the scroll, rolled it up, and set it aside, then turned to Lias. He seemed genuinely surprised to see Lias was awake.

"My goodness, you are not one to surrender easily, are you?"

"I hurt…" Lias managed to whisper.

"I should imagine you do. Well, I can help with that."

"Why? Why are you helping me? You are a knight. I am a slave…"

"You may rest assured it is not because I make it a habit to side with those who abuse my friends. Necromis seems to think you have some merit. Frankly, had you struck *me* with a chamber pot and accused me of having dealings with Bonecracker, your grave would be cooling as we speak. I am here because Necromis asked me to tend to you. Which is fine with me as it gives me a chance to ask you about the phantom nursemaid, Bonnifas."

"She was no phantom. She was real. So real I could smell her. Like dead meat."

Hawthorne walked to a delicate writing table and seated himself before it. Lias watched as he opened an ornate wooden box and drew out some small leather bags.

"She smelled of rancid flesh?" inquired Hawthorne as he began blending ingredients from the bags in a small silver bowl.

"Yes. Like spoiled meat. It was vile. Why? Does that mean something?"

Hawthorne glanced to the open window. Lias noticed that the light had changed; it appeared the sun was beginning to sink.

"It may explain a great deal," said Hawthorne, turning his attention back to the powders he was blending. "Tonight is the first of three nights of the duppy."

"Puppy?" inquired Lias.

"No, not puppy. Duppy. An evil entity with many forms. I wonder now if it was not the duppy in form of the nursemaid."

"I have never heard of this creature."

"Few have," said Hawthorne. "But every third full moon, it shows itself for three nights. The first is the night of storms, then the night of no moon, and then the night of the dead. It vanishes then for three months. Tonight is the night of storms, so even if Necromis had not asked me to stay, chances are I would have anyway. The storms of the duppy are not to be taken lightly."

"The dark is falling very fast," said Lias as the room filled with an eerie golden light. Dark clouds were beginning to fill the sky, bringing about an early twilight.

"Yes, well, as I said, the storms of the duppy are no small thing. It is another creature we would end if we could catch it."

In the distance, Lias thought he heard the bawl of a small calf. Hawthorne began grinding the powders with a little more aggression.

"Hearken to the siren song of a monster, dressed as a lost little calf."

The calf bawled again, sounding sad and afraid. Hawthorne finished mixing and grinding the powder, then dumped it into a cup of wine mixed with water. He carried it over to Lias and urged him to drink it.

"This will ease your pain."

"So it is poison, then, because only death can ease this hurt."

"Drink the wine."

Lias did, though he had no hope it would grant any relief. He then ate a few mouthfuls of bread, listening as the bawling grew closer. Slowly, the pain ebbed, and he found his breathing eased, and he felt stronger. He looked to Hawthorne as he sat at the desk, writing busily on a scrap of paper, seemingly oblivious to the noise of the calf.

"I wish to see it," said Lias quietly.

"See what?"

"The duppy. I wish to see the creature that tricked me."

"Lias, you are in no shape to get to the window."

Lias fell silent. He knew Hawthorne was right. Just because he did not hurt so much now did not mean he was not badly hurt. Still, he wished to see this thing that had gained him a beating. Carefully, slowly, with great pain and effort, Lias got to his unsteady feet while Hawthorne watched.

"You say you were a blacksmith?"

"Woodsman."

"Funny, I would swear your head is made of iron, but trees are hard, too."

"I wish to see it. So I will see it."

Hawthorne watched as Lias slowly, painfully, toddled across the floor, moving at a speed that a snail could outpace. Then he rolled his eyes and rose to his feet.

"Oh, let me help. By the time you make it to the window, it will be coming again for the second time."

Lias did not wish to be touched or helped but voiced no objection when Hawthorne came to his side. He made it to the window in time to see the creature and sat carefully on the wide ledge to look down at the beast. Far below, he saw a small calf dragging a length of chain far too large for such a little animal, bawling piteously.

"It is but a calf," said Lias. "As I suspected."

"Is it indeed?" asked Hawthorne.

He walked over to the desk and picked up a small bit of bread left on a plate. He carried it over to the window and tossed it down, the soft matter striking the calf. Lias

54

gasped as the creature looked up, its eyes blackened pits of fire and flames licking out of its mouth.

"But... I would have sworn...!"

"The Orders of Knights that are here, *are* here for this very reason," said Hawthorne softly. "This land is cursed with many foul creatures. We seek them, we slay them, and they, in turn, do the same to us. Do I believe that you sat here and were told something unspeakable by a nurse maid who smelled of death? Yes, I do. However, do I believe that what it said was true? Not for a moment. You had not been here long enough to know of the darkness that prowls this area, so you were easy to trick. Do I believe Necromis would kill a slave in sacrifice to Bonecracker? No. Never. I would throw myself from this very window if ever I thought that, for I would know then nothing good can be true."

"Everyone seems to think very highly of him," said Lias.

"Necromis is a *good man*," said Hawthorne softly and emphatically. "He has odd habits, but that is all they are—odd. And his obsession with angry slaves is because he cannot forgive himself for what became of his only love. Your new master is somewhat peculiar, I will concur. But he is not evil."

"That will hardly save me now," said Lias. "If I go back to the slave trader in my current shape, I'll only feed the dogs."

"He may not send you back."

"Why would he keep me now?"

"Well, I would not," said Hawthorne. "But I am not Necromis."

The door opened, and in walked Necromis, still beautiful despite the gash on his face. He stopped and stared at Lias with a rage that sucked the very warmth from the room.

"Hawthorne, would you leave us, please?" asked Necromis.

Hawthorne did. Lias sat on the window ledge, unable to flee, or defend himself, or do anything in the event this man decided to lash out. Perhaps sensing blood, the calf below bawled monstrously, as if hoping for flesh. For a long time, Lias and Necromis looked at each other. Then Necromis turned away to cross the room and pick up a long polearm from a rack mounted to the wall.

"You are angry, and you have lost much," said Necromis. "But I have lost much, too, and I will not suffer abuse at the hands of an ungrateful brat."

Lias watched as Necromis turned, holding the long polearm. Far below, the calf made a freakish yowling sound. Lias suddenly realized there was a very good chance he was about to be shoved out the window, and whatever lie Necromis made up to tell his friends would not be questioned. He was, after all, only a slave. And he was hardly in any condition to run away.

"I'm sorry," whispered Lias.

"I am sorry, what was that what you said? It sounded like a feeble attempt to save your own neck."

"Hawthorne told me of the creatures that surround this castle," said Lias, realizing he was actually afraid for his life for the first time in a long time. Why was that? Was it because, somehow, a tiny seed of hope had germinated in his heart?

"And I am expected to believe that never before had you heard tell of them," said Necromis.

"I am from the southern lands," said Lias. "We hear of the knights of the north and the monsters they battle, but none who come to tell the tales dare speak of the creatures for fear they will come when they hear their names uttered. No, I had not heard of these things."

"You certainly were quick enough to accuse *me* of evil! And now you go from cold iron to a whining worm. Well, I will not throw you out the window, though my heart yearns to feed you to the rolling calf. I will do worse. I will take you back to the trader."

Back to the chains and the shit and the rot. It would be a slow and hard death indeed.

"Then I choose to cast myself from the window," said Lias.

He slowly turned, intending to throw himself to the ground far below, but he could hardly move with any great speed. Then he felt the hook of the polearm catch the back of his tunic and pull him into the room.

"I didn't give you permission to kill yourself," said Necromis sharply.

"Hardly to be wondered at since I did not ask!" Lias managed to say, teeth ground in pain.

Lias was dragged across the gleaming floor with frictionless ease by Necromis, back to his bed. The tall knight placed him on it, then arranged the blankets around him. Lias' mind briefly strayed to the thought of how much he would miss this soft mattress and clean sheets.

"Now lie there and try to behave yourself. I pity your mother. Your antics as a child must have turned her grey before her time."

"And what did your parents do? Rejoice as they watched their son chase the coat tails of other men?"

"My father cared not what I chased so long as I produced no bastards and was awake when he called upon me for work. I succeeded in both rather admirably."

"That is no great feat where two men are concerned."

"He only told me not to *produce* bastards, he did not question my methods in *preventing* them." Necromis chained him to the wall once more.

"Unnatural freak," snarled Lias.

"Better a freak than a fool too stupid to accept an opportunity to save his own neck," said Necromis. "By this time tomorrow, you will be wishing you were here."

Yes, that was very true, and it seemed Necromis was well past the point of no return when it came to Lias' antics. Only then did Lias realize how bloody stupid he had been. This man could help him find his wife and only wished to

57

indulge a warped fantasy of saving a dead lover. He was snatching his own horrible slow death from the very jaws of life.

"Do not send me back, I pray!" he suddenly beseeched with a terror and grief that lunged out of him like a desperate animal.

Necromis stepped back, surprised by the outburst, shaking his head as if the force of the words stunned him.

"Please," whispered Lias. "I swear I'll behave. Only do not send me back there to die."

Necromis gazed down at him. In the distance, the calf bawled. Then Necromis put the chain around Lias' neck once more; a newer, far lighter chain, but a chain all the same.

"I will think on this," he said. "I promise nothing."

Chapter Five

The storm worsened as the evening wore on. After Necromis had chained Lias to the wall once more, he had then gone down to the pool to drink wine and soak in the heated waters, naked. Lias could see him reflected in the polished silver of a great bear statue that formed part of a pillar outside the window, as well as the distant woods where the flames of Bonecracker's fire rose higher, bidding welcome to the other evil things in this world.

The bawling of the rolling calf could still be heard, and as the storm began to tear at the castle like a mad thing, the air became sickeningly warm and humid. This was the sort of storm that heralded the end of lives, yet Necromis relaxed in his pool, watching the trees whip and the rain lash as if he were at the theatre. Did the man not know fear?

Lias scooted farther away from the window, at least as far as his chain allowed. The calf sounded closer, but Lias had no way, and no inclination, to look out the window. He hated Necromis for leaving the damned window open. He hated the man for a lot of reasons, but as the sounds of the calf grew louder, Lias realized being alone right now topped his list.

Slowly, as he cringed and shook, occasionally looking to the pillar to see the knight reflected there, he realized he did not hate him. He wanted to — oh, how he longed to despise him. But Necromis was his only hope of finding Merdine, and it was for her sake that he had to behave himself. He swore to any good and decent gods listening that if Necromis did not take him back to the trader, he would humble himself and try to be this strange knight's friend. For Merdine. Only for Merdine.

The calf bawled, no longer attempting to hide its otherworldly origins. Odd how it seemed to be under the window. Then there came a peculiar, worrying noise; a sort of eerie scraping, almost as if something hooved was climbing the wall. The chain clinked, and the sound drew nearer.

Heart pounding, Lias tugged at his own chain. Fear swept through him as the sounds outside the window continued, as if climbing the stone wall. The metal rubbed his skin, cutting into it as desperation set in and he struggled to get free. He didn't dare look up at the window. Didn't want to know or see if the rolling calf waited for him just outside. He began praying quietly, pride warring with fear. If he screamed, would anyone even hear him? Would any come to aid a slave who scarred a man as beloved as Necromis?

The sound drew closer, scraping, scratching, the tone of the bawling taking on a hellish note. There came a brief flash of movement, then another as a freakish hoof, now showing long, rusted nails thrusting out of it like makeshift claws, came into view. It caught the stone ledge of the window, and then appeared a monstrous bloody head, parts of the skull showing red through the flesh, flames drooling from the nose and mouth. It stared straight at Lias.

Then the bloody horror smiled at him.

Pride be damned.

Lias screamed. He renewed his struggle against the chain, blood welling from the cuts the collar had made. The calf slithered through the window like a corpse on a string. As the beast began moving toward him, its grotesque hooves sparking along the floor, Lias bellowed at the top of his lungs. He didn't give a damn anymore about how much he hated Necromis. He prayed to every deity he could think of that the man—or anyone—would hear him.

There were worse things than death, and he was looking at one now.

The door flew open, and there appeared a soaking wet figure, nude, with a goblet of wine in one hand. Necromis looked at Lias as if wondering why the man was shrieking as if he had lost what was left of his mind, then looked to the window. He stared at the rolling calf as it wailed and spit flame, then set down his wine and picked up his sword from the rack where it was stored.

"You dare violate *my* sanctuary, monster? Come for *my* slave? He may be worth little, but he is *mine*, and only *I* decide his fate!"

The creature lunged, and Necromis met it, taking an injury almost immediately, the rusty iron claws slashing his thigh. Enraged, Necromis brought the sword down, splitting the monster's skull to little avail.

Lias froze, unable to look away. The attack only seemed to anger the calf and made it more grotesque. The stench of rotting meat made Lias retch. The calf stumbled backward, and Lias drew himself into a ball to avoid one of the beast's demonic hooves, hoping — praying — the man could kill this damned creature.

The mutilated monster reared, belching flames with a hot vile stench like dead animals and sulphur. The claws scraped Necromis' flesh, and again the knight swung his sword, this time shouting out a word. The weapon flared with blue fire, and suddenly the image of a gigantic white bear wrought of light appeared. It slammed the calf to the stone floor with one mighty paw, and Necromis brought the sword down with a sickening crunch of bone. The monster screamed, split now into halves. Necromis set down the sword and picked up a piece of the calf by one leg and threw it out the window. The bear vanished with a soft fragrant cloud, and Necromis threw the second half of the creature out the window after the first. It still bawled, but the sound was far weaker. Almost sad.

Shaking from his head to his toes, Lias remained where he sat, huddled into a ball, eyes wide in shock. Even if he could find his voice, he had no words for what he'd witnessed. He finally managed to blink, even though he couldn't actually move any other part of his body at the moment.

"Thank you," he whispered, so low he doubted Necromis even heard it.

Necromis went to his sword, picking it up and cleaning it, his white skin marred by claw marks. "What is

61

this I hear? A murmur of gratitude? I should think you were cheering for the calf. Ugh. Look at this mess."

The door opened, and Hawthorne burst in, clearly half asleep and only partly dressed.

"My darling, you have come to rescue me!" said Necromis as Hawthorne stared at the swathe of blood across the floor.

Lias looked Necromis up and down, noting every wound. The blood — mostly the calf's — had gotten everywhere, including on Necromis' normally pristine, pale skin.

"You're hurt," Lias said. He immediately winced at stating the obvious. He chalked it up to fearing for his life moments before.

Necromis and Hawthorne both slowly turned their heads to look at him.

"Yes," said Necromis, as if addressing a not-very-bright toddler. "It had big scary claws."

"Shall I dress your wounds?" asked Hawthorne.

"I have a better idea," purred Necromis. "Let's undress yours and see whose is bigger." He waggled his eyebrows suggestively.

Hawthorne pet Necromis' head gently. "Good night, Necromis."

"Hardly, without you."

Hawthorne left. With his departure, the room settled into a somewhat awkward silence while Necromis cleaned up. Lias watched him.

"I meant what I said. Thank you."

Necromis gave him a hard look, as if he did not especially believe him. The injury on his cheek was still red and angry, and now he was injured anew on Lias' behalf. Merrigale arrived just then with several other servants to clean up the mess. None reacted to Necromis' nudity. Apparently, their lord and master running about naked was nothing new to them. The blood was cleaned, a bath drawn, and then Necromis and Merrigale had a brief conversation, something to do with the lower storerooms showing signs of flooding. She and the other servants departed, and Necromis settled into the bath to clean his wounds. It was only when they were alone again that Necromis spoke to Lias.

"I will be succinct. I tried to be kind to you and received an injury on my face that I shall never forgive. Were it received in battle, I would dismiss it, but you shouted obscenities at me then hurled a pot of shit. I cannot say that returning you to the slave trader does not hold a great deal of appeal for me right this moment, especially after you declared me to be one who pays homage to Bonecracker."

Lias looked away. Having seen what awaited him outside these walls, he realized it could be worse - *much* worse than anything Necromis had yet done to him, whipping included. He could never erase what he'd said, and he wasn't sure he wanted to — yet. But if he didn't find a way to change Necromis' mind about getting rid of him, Lias knew death would be his only option. He forced himself to look at Necromis, to endure the man's unnerving gaze.

"I… I am sorry."

The burning green eyes seemed to stare right through his flesh. They seemed to emit an eerie light in the dimly lit room. Finally, Necromis spoke again.

"Lias, this game we are playing is very simple. You will respect me. You will understand that my sense of humour regarding any antics you care to perpetrate is gone. You will take to heart the warning that one more outburst from you *will* result in the end of your life. And any more lies about me *willingly paying homage* to Bonecracker will result in you *becoming* an homage to Bonecracker."

Lias swallowed and nodded. "I understand."

"Good. Now you will lie there, and you will heal." The storm slammed the shutters closed, and Necromis sighed. "And you have another reason to lay low and quiet. The rolling calf has seen you and marked you for his own. Do not think he is dead. He is not. We do not know yet how to kill him. We know only that those he has come for with a purpose are in danger."

63

A chill stole over Lias, and he shivered. He glanced at the shuttered window. Then he looked back to Necromis. "What if he comes again? Can he get inside?"

"Yes, of course, it can come inside. You just saw it do so for yourself. But never fear." Necromis' voice became cold. "The preening pretty boy who primps like a woman will save you. You know — the one who brought you out of the death-hole where you were left to die and to whom you have shown *so* much gratitude. "

Necromis was clearly still angry, and it was unlikely he had abandoned the idea of just killing Lias anyway. Lias began to regret those particular words. Pretty or not, Necromis had more than proven that he was not weak or cowardly in the least.

Lias ignored the fact that the man was fully nude as he stepped, wet and gleaming, out of the bath. He'd never met another man who cared so little if others saw him in such a state. If he was going to save his neck, Lias knew he'd have to swallow a bit more pride.

"What can I do or say to convince you that I am sincere?"

"Damned little at this point!" snapped Necromis. "Even when I had dared hope for a moment you had found your civility, you ruin my face! The only grace I will grant you at this moment is not dragging you back from whence you came, but you best keep in mind the option remains." Necromis reached for a towel. He began drying himself and preparing for what seemed to be his evening ritual. He seated himself at his vanity and began oiling and braiding his damp hair. When he spoke again, his voice was more gentle.

"I do not expect you to understand my motives," said Necromis. "Few do."

Lias studied Necromis. A part of him wondered why Necromis had bought him in the first place. He was nothing special and certainly not a stable boy, as Necromis' former love had been. Necromis, for all his preening, was a very pretty man, if one were interested in such appearances

64

in their men. Why buy slaves when he could have someone much better? None of it made much sense.

"If I asked you what such motives were, would you tell me?"

Necromis was carefully oiling his hair, making it clear that his appearance meant a great deal to him. "I see no reason why not. You could learn the tale from any of my servants, or dear Hawthorne, though be warned, he does not care for you much right now, either. I was in love with a stable boy. His name was Sterling. I sacrificed... far more than you will ever know to have him. But he was murdered. Childish as it may sound, I cannot rest until I feel that I have in some way made it up to him. Earned his forgiveness." He tossed his head, showing a brief flash of rage and pain in the gesture. "But you know how emotional men like myself are."

Lias winced at the dig. He had been most unfair to this man. He wound up here because his own love had been taken and sold as a slave. He didn't know if she lived, but it didn't change how he felt. A part of him understood how Necromis felt. What did one say in such a situation? Lias had no idea how to respond.

"I..." He shook his head, at a loss for words. "I do not know what to say except... I am sorry."

Necromis finished grooming, then rose to his feet. He walked to a cabinet, took out an elaborately embroidered housecoat, and wrapped it about himself. "Spare me your grovelling, it does not suit you. I said I would not send you back. What more do you want?"

Then he departed, leaving the room, as well as a plate of food within reach for Lias. Once more, it was good food, not slop. Even in his anger, Necromis did not feed garbage to his slave.

Lias sighed. He had no way of convincing Necromis that he'd been sincere, and why would the man believe him? He'd just gone from rage and loathing to trying to save his own neck, and Necromis was clearly not an idiot. He would know there was a rather *large* level of *in*sincerity in what

Lias said. All right, yes, he was trying to save his own skin and find his wife, and he deeply suspected there was some truth to the accusation of Necromis paying homage to Bonecracker—that look on his face when Lias accused him had been stark staring terror. But… there did seem to be goodness in him as well.

He tugged the plate closer and began nibbling. Before long, his body reminded him how starved he'd been before Necromis found him. He made himself eat slowly, though. No sense in being a pig only to have it all come back up. As he ate, he studied the room, hoping to find something—anything—that he could use to find at least a tiny hint of common ground with his… What was Necromis to him? Owner? Captor? Lias honestly didn't know. No captor would have risked life and limb to save him. In Lias' experience, no owner would have either.

Lias finished eating and sat back against the wall. "He hates me. Not that I blame him," Lias muttered to himself. "No wonder he doesn't believe a word I say, sincere or not."

The door opened, and Hawthorne shuffled in, yawning. He paused and looked to the window as the wind pounded against the shutters, forcing drops of rain sideways into the room.

"Miserable night," he muttered, then looked to Lias. "And how are you?"

"I've been better," Lias answered. He sighed. "I made a very big mistake. Now I don't know how to fix it."

"Which one?" asked Hawthorne dryly.

Lias grimaced. "Point taken. All of them, really." He stared down at the empty plate. No other owner had ever fed him such things. No other owner had ever risked their life to save his. Necromis, much to Lias' chagrin, was proving to be like no one he'd ever met. "I expected Necromis to be no different from the others. Therefore, I treated him with the same hatred. But he isn't like the others. Nothing I can say will ever convince him that I was wrong."

"I've an idea," said Hawthorne, seating himself on the floor beside Lias' humble bed, clipping away some of the old bandages. "Why don't you try using actions, not words? Radical things like not pissing on his tapestries, or throwing your own waste, or declaring him a servant of Bonecracker? Had you said that to me, you would not be alive to regret your actions. But I can only assume the duppy was playing with your emotions. That is the sort of thing it would do."

Lias wanted nothing more than to sink into the floor and never return. He'd been raised much better than that. He'd taught his daughters much better than that. Had he really let his hatred rule him to the point where he lost his humanity?

"Before I was taken, before... all of this, I raised my children to be strong but kind. I didn't raise them to behave like animals. It shames me to know that I fell to such depths. I can't take back my actions, but I can promise that I will not repeat them. I am not an educated man, but I'm not stupid."

"You will forgive us if we do not take you at your word."

The door creaked open, and moments later, a white face with a black muzzle peered in. The gigantic horse snuffled the air, then plodded into the room. Judging by the small scrapes on his hide, the horse had broken out of his stable in a panic, then come looking for his master for comfort. He walked over to the two men to examine them for treats.

Lias blinked up at the enormous creature. He'd never seen any horse so big in his life. Wary of his clinking chain frightening the beast, he reached up, hoping the horse would let him pet it. He'd always loved animals, big and small.

"He's beautiful."

"Rufus is a brat," grumbled Hawthorne, making a face as the animal stood over him.

Rufus sniffed Lias all over, then turned his attention to Hawthorne, sniffing him as well. Since nobody had anything that horses liked, Rufus walked over to the bed, stepping up onto it, circling once like any dog before thumping down onto the quilts and blankets. Shockingly, the bed held with hardly a squeak.

"Looks like Necromis had the frame reinforced with steel after all," Hawthorne mumbled. Something tumbled out of the bandage Hawthorne opened, and he reacted by popping a pillowcase over Lias' head.

"My goodness, all the candles blew out," said Hawthorne as he began working on the wound. It was an old one, from Lias' time in the slave trader's pit.

"What the…" Lias shook his head to try to dislodge the pillowcase. "What are you doing? Ow!"

"Just sit still, I'll deal with this," said Hawthorne. He could be felt picking carefully at the wound, then rinsing it with something cold that stung. "There. Much better." Hawthorne plucked off the case. "Oh, look, the candles lit themselves again."

Lias stared at the man, convinced Hawthorne had lost his mind. He glanced down at the newly-redressed wound, then up at Hawthorne. "I don't want to know, do I?"

"No, you don't, trust me. Now, did you eat all your nummies?" Hawthorne drew a gasp as he saw Lias' empty plate. "My goodness, you did, what a good boy! Now, if I leave you alone for five minutes to see where your master is, do you think you and the horse can behave?"

The horse emitted a fart that rivaled the storm outside, startling itself awake. The air took on a scent of rotting apples, decomposing hay, and old swamp weeds.

"Farewell, Lias, I shall speak well of you at your funeral." Hawthorne fled the horse-fart.

Lias choked and gagged, too busy struggling to breathe to answer. His eyes watered, and he scowled at the horse. He slapped one hand across his nose and mouth, muffling his words. "For such a beautiful animal, you are foul."

Rufus made a sleepy noise, closing his eyes, untroubled by his own emissions.

* * *

The storm raged, causing the candles to sputter, but the atmosphere in the castle seemed more peaceful, as if something evil had been defeated. Roughly two hours after Necromis had left the room, he returned, dressed in the padded clothing knights wore beneath their armor. He was bloodied and filthy and exhausted, his white hair in disarray, his flesh steaming from the exertion of the battle. He said nothing to Lias, but it seemed clear he had vented his rage on the rolling calf, defeating it for now. He was bent and bleeding and said nothing at all. Looking dazed, he began slowly removing the padding.

Still regretting his prior actions, Lias asked, "May I help?"

Necromis looked exhausted beyond the will to live, slowly peeling off the filthy wet garb. "The only thing I want from you is decent behaviour, and failing that, a hot rum toddy. Even if you offered yourself to me, I'd be too tired to fuck you." Necromis forced open one eye and looked at the woodsman. "*Can* you make a toddy? I mean without spitting in it or letting a live rat swim in it."

Lias blinked. Did he know how to make a hot rum toddy? It seemed so long since he had enjoyed one. "I haven't made one in quite a while, but, yes, I know how."

Necromis studied Lias for a long time, as if asking himself if he really was dumb enough to let this man off his leash. Finally, he did so. He indicated a decorative shelf filled with fine spirits.

"Make yourself one as well. Then we shall chase each other around the room to see who surrenders his virtue to whom." The knight was moving every bit as slowly as his battered slave, and as he dropped his padding, it was clear that his battle with the rolling calf had been bitter and violent indeed.

Lias slowly rose to his feet and winced when pain sparked in places he didn't remember he had. He was in no shape to be standing as he went to the shelf and found the ingredients necessary for a toddy. He mixed two drinks and

69

handed one to Necromis. When he realized just how slowly the man moved, Lias set both drinks down and approached Necromis cautiously.

"I won't… do anything," he said. "Just let me help you get the padding off."

Without giving Necromis a chance to reply, Lias began helping him, thinking they must make a fine pair — one battered and tortured, one beaten and bloody. He kept his touches as light as possible, knowing the slightest move could be painful or taken the wrong way. Necromis allowed Lias to help him with the padding, at least until it became clear the man had no idea what he was doing. This was hardly surprising, given he was a wood cutter and not a squire.

"Away with you," grumped Necromis, but with no real anger. "You'll pull my arm off. Undo the straps in the back. You'll do less damage there."

Lias chuckled softly, surprisingly himself. He couldn't remember the last time he'd laughed at all. He worked open the straps on the back. "If I hurt you, I'm sorry. I've never actually done this before."

"Oh, I love it when a man says that to me," sighed Necromis.

Lias froze for a moment. "Wait. No. I meant…" He sighed and undid the last strap. "I give up."

"You'll need a filthier mind," said Necromis, as if noting to himself what needed to be done with a troublesome machine. "The rest is fine, but you need a much dirtier mind." He tried his toddy and had some sort of fit as he did so, scrunching his face up. "By all that is unholy, how much rum did you put in this? I've drunk the flaming blood of a demon-wyvern, and it wasn't near as strong as this! Lias, if you mean to have your way with me, just ask!"

Lias spit a mouthful of toddy out, torn between choking and laughing. He hadn't thought about the fact that someone else might not enjoy their drinks quite as strong as he did. He wiped his mouth with the back of his hand while trying not to laugh anymore.

70

"I did tell you it's been a while. I've always preferred mine a bit... strong."

"Indeed?" Necromis' voice was an inviting purr. "Tell me — what else do you like strong?"

There was unmistakable sexual innuendo to the question — playful and light, to be sure, but... he was asking something, trying to learn something about Lias. He did not press his proximity, but the question... was he asking if Lias liked men?

"Uh." Lias blinked again. Surely, Necromis didn't mean... "Plows, axes. Trees. Strong horses are good, too." He held up his drink. "I especially love strong drinks."

"Those are all very fine," said Necromis softly. Then he did step closer, dirty and bleeding, his white skin showing every speck of filth. "Anything else?"

Lias took a wary step back. "Um, no. That's pretty much it." He grabbed Necromis' glass. "Need another? I need another."

Necromis smiled — a real, human smile. He turned to the bath and began refilling it. "I would like mine a little less strong. It's been a long battle, and I've not much strength left. So I take it that you've never taken a man to your bed, only women."

Lias nearly dropped one of the bottles. The mere thought made him shudder. "Never. Not to... judge you, or anything. But I have absolutely no interest in other men." He made Necromis' drink significantly less strong, but with enough rum to add a little kick. Then he turned and handed it to Necromis once the man settled into the tub.

"Just curious," said Necromis easily. He seemed cheerful, but perhaps it was the drink. "I never loved anyone other than men. One man in particular. A beautiful man who taught me many useless things, such as how to teach a horse to sleep on your bed."

Lias snorted. He glanced at the snoring horse curled up like a dog. "Surely, he won't stay there when you go to bed. Will he?"

71

"He will," said Necromis, sighing. "And I will not have the heart to put him outside in the rain. And indeed, why is he any less than I? Why should I have a warm dry bed in a safe keep whilst my dearest companion sleeps in damp hay?"

Rufus farted.

"Well, there is that," said Necromis. "Lias, you monster, I am drunk."

Lias chuckled. "If it's any consolation… so am I."

Necromis sank into the bath, gingerly picking at his wounds, slowly and carefully cleaning them. He removed from one cut a piece of rusted nail, clearly broken off from the duppy's hoof.

"It was a hard battle, and all for naught. The monster will just be back tomorrow eve."

"There has to be some way to kill it," Lias said. He finished his drink and set the glass down before sitting on his bed. "Is there anything I can do?"

Necromis gave him an odd look, as if asking himself if this was the same slave that only hours ago tried to kill him with a chamber pot. He suddenly seemed downright suspicious.

"No," he said quietly, still giving Lias that odd look. "No, I am fine. Here, a souvenir for you."

He tossed Lias the bit of duppy-iron.

Lias caught it. He stared at the nail. It didn't look like any nail he'd ever seen. "Isn't this from one of the calf's hooves?" He recalled the way sparks lit when the creature had slithered across the floor and shuddered.

"Yes, it is," said Necromis, still studying him. "All right, I confess, I am curious. Why are you being nice? Not more than twelve hours ago, you hit me with a pot full of shit. Now you are making drinks and asking questions. Who did you contact to come kill me?"

That surprised a laugh out of Lias. He set the nail down and sighed. How did he answer such a question? "I may not be educated, but I am not stupid. If you mistreat an animal, it distrusts you and lashes out, violently. When that animal finds someone who does not mistreat it, that instinct remains because it's so deeply ingrained at that point. It takes time to get out of that cycle. I realized that the only time you have been harsh to me..." Lias grimaced. "Well, I deserved it. When the duppy came after me, I thought I was dead. You saved my life. No one else had ever done such a thing before."

"That's lovely, Lias, truly. But if you don't mind, let us each hold close to our hearts a small bit of paranoia. We each have reason to fear, I think."

The storm blasted the shutters, flinging drops of rain into the room. In the distance, something that sounded like a child screaming could be heard. Then a great puff of flame rose up in the deep woods. Necromis sipped his drink and cleaned his wounds, heedless of the nightmarish sounds around him.

Lias retreated to his bed as quickly as he was able, which was by no means fast, unable to look away from the window. "That's putting it very mildly," he muttered. The unholy shriek sounded nothing like the calf. If anything, it sounded far more frightening. Lias shuddered and drew himself into a ball, sitting with his back flat against the wall. "What is that?"

"Oh, make no mistake, that was the duppy, enraged at being forced from its earthly form. You'd better brace yourself. We have two more nights of this, each worse than the last. The knights are here because the evil is here."

There came a tap on the door, and Merrigale poked her head in. "You have company my lord."

"You're drunk," exclaimed Necromis.

Merrigale was indignant. "I am not. Some fool by the name of Sir Barton is..."

"Oh, by all the gods and bears that are! What is that idiot doing out on one of the three nights of the duppy?"

"Getting his foolish self lost by the looks of it," said Merrigale.

Lias glanced at Necromis. "Who is Sir Barton?"

"A moron," said Necromis flatly. "Bait for bears and nothing more. Send him away. No! Wait! I will speak with him. Then I am going to bed. I've had a damned long night and am in no mood for idiots!"

Necromis slowly and painfully dragged himself out of the bath, wrapped himself in a robe, and limped out of the room. Merrigale began cleaning up the blood, spilled water, and towels.

Lias watched for a moment before speaking. "He's not like the others."

"What others?" inquired Merrigale, busily cleaning. She seemed to be able to do so at an astounding speed.

"The ones who bought me before him. Necromis is nothing like them." Lias watched her in awe. "How can you do that so quickly yet so thoroughly?"

"Practice," she said dryly. "And no, he is nothing at all like any other man. One day, he will find a proper man to love, take in children to raise as heirs, and become king. And we will all be better for it. How *dare* you accuse him of paying homage to Bonecracker! Lie down, rest yourself. Do you want to undo all of Sir Hawthorne's work?"

Lias barely stopped himself from saying 'yes, ma'am.' He stretched out on his bed. "I told him I was sorry, and I will repeat it to you. I said such things out of anger, but he did not deserve the accusations."

"No, he did not! What are you wearing? It's filthy." She had Lias out of his nightshirt in a second and was shoving a fresh one over his head.

Lias grumbled until the shirt slipped down to cover him. "I'm not a child, you know. I am capable of dressing myself." He glanced at the tub. "If I might ask, could I possibly wash soon?"

"You cannot wash until your wounds heal a little more. But I will bring you a cloth and a basin, and you can attend to yourself."

"Thank you," Lias said quietly.

Merrigale brought him a basin and a cloth, then he was left to his own devices. An hour later, Necromis stumbled in, walked directly to his bed, and fell onto it, sleeping beside his horse, one arm thrown across the mighty animal's neck.

Lias finished washing, being as quiet as possible. He cleaned as much as he could before he had to stand to take off the nightshirt. His wounds looked awful, but he'd been through much worse. He wet the cloth and dabbed at a few of the larger wounds. He wished he could wash his hair, but doing so would have required far more water, soap, and noise. A snort came from the bed, and he glanced over, no clue if the sound came from his host or the animal in the man's bed.

"Psst," said a voice from the window.

Lias grabbed his nightshirt and tugged it on. "Who's there?" he whispered.

A skinny arm in a nursemaid's pink-striped sleeve wriggled under the window shutter and waved. Moments later, a huge eye and skull-like face could be seen. "Did you tell him about the present I gave you?"

Lias stumbled backward, tripping over the basin and spilling water onto the floor. The creature smiled, a grotesque expression that sent a chill racing up Lias' spine.

"You," he muttered. "What are you? What do you want?"

"I'm the nursemaid, silly. You met me earlier! I watch all the invisible babies! Would you like to know where Sir Barton is?"

Lias shook his head, heart thundering. "No. Leave me alone. You don't belong here, you don't work here. I don't know what or who you really are, but I want nothing from you."

She giggled, then chanted in a sing-song vice, "He's in the basement, he's in the meat locker, he's going to be sacrificed... How lucky for you that Necromis needs you alive. He needs your warm willing flesh..."

"I don't believe you," Lias shot back. "Get out!"

She grinned at him. "Oh, don't be scared, poor Lias! After he's had your strong young body beneath his own, he will kill you kindly, I am sure!"

"Leave me alone!" Lias shouted. "I'd just as soon lay beneath him before I ever believe a word you say, demon!"

"Lias…" said Necromis sleepily, "not that the idea of laying with you is not attractive, but why are you shouting at the window?"

"You don't see her? How can you not see her? She's right there, in the window! The demon who claimed to be a nursemaid."

Necromis slowly turned his head to look to the window, staring at the creature leaning through the shutters. He scowled. The demon nursemaid waved.

"Hi."

"For the love of all the gods, do you know what time it is? I'm tired. Leave my slave alone. He's had enough for one day. For that matter, so have I, so be gone. We can all be held in awe by your hideous visage later."

Necromis rolled over and pulled the blankets up.

"You're no fun," sulked the demon.

"Not at two in the bloody morning, I'm not," muttered Necromis.

Lias' jaw dropped open. He gaped at the Necromis-shaped lump on the bed, then at the demon lady in the window. Thoroughly confused, he flopped down onto his bed. "Just…" He closed his eyes. "Just go. Please. This has to be a dream."

"Would you like a bedtime story?" crooned the demon.

"Lias, why don't you show the nice monster your piece of duppy-iron?" asked Necromis.

The monster shrieked and fled.

Lias blinked. "How…?" He picked up the piece of iron nail and studied it before looking back at the window. "Demons are afraid of iron?"

Necromis shifted to get comfortable. "Forged and meteoric iron do ugly things to preternatural creatures, duppy-iron especially. It is iron from the deepest bowels of the netherworlds, forged *by* demons to inflict pain *on* demons. Keep it close. And go to sleep."

"Right," Lias muttered. Clutching the piece of iron close, he lay down. "Good night, Necromis."

"Shut up and let me sleep," grumbled the knight.

Lias held the iron tight in his fist and closed his eyes.

Chapter Six

Morning came too damn early. Lias almost had to force his eyes open. The night had been long and rather frightening, in entirely too many ways. He held up the piece of iron nail that he'd clutched all night long, gazing at it in wonder. Maybe if he made it into a pendant, the nursemaid demon would leave him alone. There wasn't much he could do about the duppy, but, according to Necromis, demons couldn't touch iron—especially duppy iron. It gave Lias a bit of security from one demon, at least.

"Necromis?" he whispered from where he still lay on his bed, unsure if the man was even awake yet. For all he knew, Necromis had already awakened and gone out to do... whatever the knight did. "Necromis, are you there?"

"Noooo..." whined the knight. "I'm dead."

Rufus the horse got off the bed, plodded across the floor, pulled open the bedroom door, and left. Lias stared at the door, one eyebrow raised. This entire household was a bit... odd. Apparently, that included the animals. Lias shook his head.

"Well, can your ghost help me make this iron nail into a pendant, please? I'd feel... safer, at least where the nursemaid demon is concerned."

Necromis slowly sat up. He looked like something risen from the dead. His white skin showed every scrape and bruise, and his pretty face was blackened. He moved like one who was in great pain. The knight tried to stand. Then he lay down once more.

"Later," he whispered.

Lias grimaced. "Do you need me to get Hawthorne?" he asked, though he had no idea how or where to find the man to begin with, assuming he could walk that far himself. "Or is there anything else I can do? You look... well... awful."

Necromis closed his eyes and seemed to sink into the mattress. It became clear very soon that he was not asleep. He was unconscious.

"Shit."

Lias got up and hissed in pain. His wounds were better, but they were far from healed. Still, he couldn't just sit there while Necromis was much worse. He got to the door, slowly, and opened it. Doors on either side led to other rooms he'd yet to see, but he figured he'd find someone eventually. He glanced back at Necromis, still as death on the bed. Then he ventured out into the hall and stopped at the first door he came to.

The room was strange to say the least. There was a basin mounted on a stand, as well as an enormous hand-painted and decorated tub mounted to the floor. A pump stood to one end to dispense water into the bath, and a grate of coals underneath the tub would heat the water. Stranger still was an odd little ceramic chair with water in the bottom, and a handle that released the water into the darkened depths of the unknown. Great mirrors adorned the room, and stained-glass windows left images of birds and flowers in coloured light on the floor.

Lias approached the chair and peered into it. "What in the world…?"

"Lias, are you escaping? Because if you are, then I can assure you that the stool-basin is not the exit you wish to use." The voice was Hawthorne's.

"What?" Lias turned around. "Uh, no. I'm going to assume, given your statement, that this is akin to a privy." He glanced at the 'stool-basin,' then backed away a bit. "I was looking for you, actually."

"I'm not down there," said Hawthorne dryly.

Lias rolled his eyes. "I gathered that. Necromis is…" He sighed. "I don't know, exactly. I know he was in pain, but he only spoke for a moment this morning and then just… nothing. Can you come see him?"

"Only if you go lie on your bed and stay still. Tell me the truth. Your wife was not stolen; she fled your nonsense."

Lias shook his head. "No, but she often accused me of being rather stubborn."

79

"Fancy that—I cannot imagine why. To your bed. Now let us see to Necromis."

Moments after Hawthorne looked at Necromis, the shutters and drapes were closed, the whole house took on a feeling of fear and worry, and Lias was in a small room of his own. No one bothered to explain anything to Lias, but it was clear Necromis was dangerously ill.

* * *

For days, Lias lay in his own bed in his own room, slowly healing, while not more than a few feet away, Necromis fought a vengeful fever that threatened to destroy him. Hawthorne had not left the castle once, and Lias sensed others were coming to see how Necromis was faring. If he was to judge by the way one morning Hawthorne drugged him with the lichen and then locked the door to his room, even the king himself had made the trip to see his intended heir. It was not a long journey, but given the health of the man, it was a gesture that truly demonstrated his love for his favoured knight.

* * *

It had been over three weeks, and while Lias was by no means well, he found he could not stay in bed one more moment. He itched to leave the room, to find Hawthorne and ask what was going on. Then again, he didn't think he really had any right to ask anyway. He sighed and sat on his bed. Head falling back against the wall, he closed his eyes.

"Just don't let him die," he muttered.

Merrigale bustled in with a meal for Lias, glaring at him, in no mind for his hard-headedness. "Bed! Now! Lie down! The master may be dying, and no one has time for your foolishness!"

"Dying?" Lias dutifully lay down, but worry set in. "Can anyone do anything? Hawthorne? Another healer? Necromis can't die!"

Merrigale gave him a very, very hard look. "Indeed, and what do you care? You who have accused him of consorting with demons?"

Lias sighed and dragged his hands down his face. "I don't know why I care," he said. "But I do. I apologized for what I said, to him, to you, to anyone who would listen."

"Then eat your dinner and stay on your bed, lest you find yourself needing a healer as well. But I must say — I've seen you looking far worse."

"Yes, ma'am," Lias answered. He glanced at Merrigale. "I am sorry, for what it's worth."

Merrigale gave him a sour look. "You certainly are. Now mind your manners, if you can. His Lordship's friends will be coming 'round to visit. I have a full house and no time for nasty slaves! Necromis said the blacksmith was to come up and help you make a pendant."

"Then he is awake?"

"Somewhat, though why he concerns himself with you, I am sure I do not know."

Lias just nodded. Nothing he said made any difference. "Thank you."

"Eat!" she grumbled and departed.

Another woman thrust her head into the room. She smelled of the forge, and her white skin was streaked with soot. "I am looking for the nastiest slave ever to walk. Is that you?"

"Apparently," Lias grumbled. He sat up and gave the blacksmith the best smile he could muster, given that his aches and pains decided to rear their ugly heads again. "Thank you for coming."

"Do not thank me. I've heard not a single good word about you, and it is your fault Necromis is sick. So save your false smiles and charm. I do this only for Necromis." She crossed the room to him and seated herself on the floor near his pallet. "Show me your nail."

Just as she spoke, a great bearded man who looked like a lion entered the room, dressed as a knight and smelling of drink.

"Is this Necromis' latest pet? You would think he would at least buy the pretty slaves to win over, but no, they all look like rabid beasts."

81

"I give up," Lias grumbled. He handed the blacksmith the iron nail and glanced at the door. The man absolutely reeked. Lias gave the knight a slight smile, even though he figured it'd do no good. "How can I help?" he asked the blacksmith, although he doubted he'd get an even remotely friendly answer. He hated being helpless.

"You can help by not spitting or biting," she said quietly, examining the nail. "Silver, I think, and a few touches of gold, along with dragon scale to bind. I will return." She gave him back the nail and left.

The knight stared down at Lias. He was clearly drunk, and there was something that spoke of poor health, but he was not cruel. "I wish I could beg you to give him what he seeks, but human hearts do not work that way," said the man softly, almost to himself.

Lias studied the man for a moment before speaking. "What does he seek?"

"I don't know," said the knight, seating himself heavily in a chair. "Some strange sort of redemption. Five slaves he has raised to fine health and usefulness, though you are by far his hardest task to date. All for the love and forgiveness of one slave. Necromis never forgave himself for failing Sterling. The spear in his heart festers and eats at him. But my manners fail me. I am Sir Blassard, Necromis' uncle. Not by blood but love."

For the first time, Lias felt like someone actually wanted to talk *to* him, instead of *down* to him. "I am Lias," he said. "It's a pleasure to meet you, Sir Blassard. Necromis has told me of his late love and what happened." Lias sighed and stared down at the nail in his hand. "When I came here, I hated him. Just like I'd hated every other person who has bought me. I've made mistakes, said and done things to Necromis that I wish I had not. I've apologized to him and to anyone else who was offended on his behalf. I never wished him ill, not when I realized he wasn't like the others." Lias laughed softly. "I am sorry. I didn't mean to burden you with my troubles, not while Necromis is so gravely ill."

82

Blassard sighed heavily, then patted him on the shoulder. "We are all gravely ill, boy. Make no mistake. We all are."

Blassard shoved a full tankard of ale into Lias' hands and left the room. Like most beer brewed by the local craftspeople, it was herbed and fragrant, with bits of grain and fruit in it. The scent was like the lemons in the groves of his home, and the colour like sun through a window, with tiny dots of colour from the herbs that gave it flavour.

Lias took a sip. It tasted like no other beer he'd ever had. He continued drinking, slowly, while he waited for the blacksmith to return. His mind, inevitably, wandered to thoughts of Necromis. Despite the troubles they'd had before, Lias worried about Necromis. He didn't wish the man any bad luck, much less bad health. Lias finished the beer and set the mug down. Head falling back against the wall, he closed his eyes while he sat on his bed, waiting. A part of him wondered if he and Necromis would ever be actual friends. He snorted. Necromis would never trust him to such an extent, and Lias wasn't sure he could do the same. Not right now, anyway, but it didn't mean he wasn't concerned about the man's well-being.

The blacksmith returned with her own slave. He was pretty and clean, his hair brushed, his skin unmarked by scars save those that any apprentice would pick up in the course of learning his trade. He was likely no more than eighteen and carried his mistress' equipment. About his neck was a fine leather collar set with beads of mother-of-pearl. That meant he was highly trusted — enough so he could come and go freely when his time was his own. His hands were already strong and large from hard work, and he smiled as he prepared the room's hearth to become a make-shift forge.

Lias snorted. The slave seemed perfectly content with such a life of constant servitude, and he was far too pristine for even a blacksmith's pack mule. A whore. That must be the slave's real duty to the blacksmith — a pretty

83

little body to warm a bed. Quick on the heels of that thought came the one that made Lias study the slave more closely.

"How old are you?"

"Hello to you, too!" retorted the boy.

"Nikas," gently chided his mistress. "Don't tease Lord Necromis' pet maniac. And keep your hands away. He bites hard enough to ruin you."

"Yes, Mistress," said Nikas. He then looked at Lias. "I'm eighteen."

Lias wrinkled his nose. "And too pretty to be a simple blacksmith slave," he muttered.

"Well, maybe if you didn't throw your own filth, piss on the floor, and bite hard enough to ruin a Seven Isles slave that cost your master a thousand reids, *you* would be pretty, too. I have a trade. What is your purpose, to feed the dogs?"

A thousand reids? Good grief why, oh, *why* had Necromis not killed him yet? That much money would be enough to make a king faint. Lias smiled slowly, the expression far from pleasant. "I'm here to remind pretty little boys like you what happens when you wear out your usefulness."

"I sincerely doubt you ever had a use," said Nikas airily. "I sincerely doubt there are any calling for the royal shit-tosser. Who would waste duppy-iron on you? It is as my mistress says: men who favour other men are all romance and foolishness. A true man would not waste such a gift on you."

"So you are saying Necromis is foolish, are you?" Lias smirked. "I'm sure he'd like to hear your thoughts."

"Oh, we all know what he's like," said Nikas. "Bends for any man that will have him, buys worthless pets, then weeps to Blassard and Hawthorne about Sterling. We all know the stories. What we don't know is why, once a month during the time of the half-moon, he walks nude through the house, covered in blood."

"Nikas!" hissed the blacksmith, and the boy fell silent.

84

Lias narrowed his gaze at the slave. Blood? He made a note to investigate such a claim, should he have the chance. "I'll be sure to ask Necromis," he said. "Of course, I shall give you full credit for the myriad questions."

"No need," said Hawthorne, who chose that moment to enter the room. "I am sure I can field any questions the boy has about *private and holy rites performed by his betters.*"

Lias bit back the urge to smirk and laugh at the uppity little slave. Instead, he sat dutifully on his bed, not daring to move lest Hawthorne chastise him. The blood issue came back to him, and Lias couldn't help but wonder what Nikas had meant. What sort of holy rite involved parading around naked and covered in blood?

Of course, with Necromis, the part about parading around naked may simply be personal preference.

Hawthorne stayed and oversaw the process of Lias' pendant being made, possibly to ensure Lias was in no way denied the powerful gift Necromis had given him. He watched as the iron was carefully beaten into shape, then bound with silver and gold infused with dust from a red dragon's scale. At last, it was hung on a chain of fine silver. The blacksmith gave it to Hawthorne, who then knelt beside Lias and carefully fastened the gift about his neck.

"Do not thank me. I do this for Necromis. Thank him."

"Thank you anyway," Lias said quietly. He touched the pendant and sighed. "Maybe it'll help."

"Suddenly all sweetness and sunshine, aren't you?" snapped the blacksmith. "That Seven Isles slave you ruined was *mine.*"

Lias paid the blacksmith no mind. He was done trying to be nice to everyone. At this point, he only wished to be civil to a handful of people. The blacksmith and her whore-slave were not on his list.

"And how did you afford a Seven Isles slave?" inquired Hawthorne. "Last I checked, a companion such as that would be beyond the price of a blacksmith, even a talented one such as yourself. Could it be that those rumours we hear of you overcharging and using inferior materials are true?"

She packed up her things and left with her slave.

Lias barely managed to keep his mouth shut. He was learning rather quickly that a slave could find out all manner of interesting things when others saw them as completely insignificant. One thing was for sure: he had a slow-growing appreciation for Hawthorne—or at least the man's bluntness. Though unsure if he would receive any sort of answer, he figured he'd try asking the one question burning in his mind.

"Nikas mentioned that Necromis walks the hall, naked and bloody. Is it a rite, or does he participate in symbolic combat of some kind?"

Hawthorne was watching after the blacksmith and her slave, as if pondering sending the guards to inspect her shop and see if his suspicions were true.

"He is of the Order of the White Bear, a powerful and secret sect. I do not question the blood-rites he performs, though I, too, have seen him in the half-light, painted with blood. Many of that order are like Necromis, though I do not know why. I do know that, on some nights, they don the skins of bears and dine on raw flesh, usually bull or boar, such as the great white bears do."

The notion intrigued Lias, though he didn't say as much. He nodded. "I've heard tales of similar rituals where I'm from, but most are legends at this point."

"You could do far worse than to let him love you," Hawthorne said, then rose to his feet as a female knight came into the room. "Lady Solecil, how good to see you."

"Is Necromis very ill?" she asked.

Hawthorne nodded. "He was injured badly doing battle with the duppy. Have you met Necromis' dainty pet? He is fragile and delicate. Do not startle him."

She gave Lias an odd look, as if wondering if this was the slave she's heard so much about—none good—and returned her gaze to Hawthorne. "Have you seen Sir Barton? His brother contacted me saying he has not seen him."

"I have not seen him, but I have not looked." Hawthorne jumped as a violent storm blew up. "And now the duppy comes. It is too late to look."

Solecil sighed in exasperation. "I thank Necromis for trying to do away with the beast, but having it return every full moon rather than every three..."

"Yes, well, I am sure he did not know. All we can do now is help him to get well."

Lias edged to the far end of his bed and stared out the window. He clutched his pendant. "Who is Sir Barton?" he asked, though most of his attention remained fixed on the shuttered window.

Sir Hawthorne briefly put his hand on Lias' head, as if gently hushing an inquisitive child. This was business for knights, not nosy slaves. He rose to his feet and walked out of the room with Lady Solecil, closing the door. Lias was now alone again.

Lias sighed. The storm outside raged on, and Lias thought he heard something ominous — evil — in the distance. He drew himself into a ball and held his pendant tight in his fist. It gave him a modicum of comfort, despite the nightmare he knew waited outside the window. He hated being confined to this room, especially when the weather got like this. Such times usually heralded demonic visits.

Instead of waiting to be tormented by any number of demons, Lias made a rather hasty decision. He got up and went to the door. Not being chained gave him freedom to move about, though he had no idea where he would go. He opened the door and peered out into the hall. He'd already found what turned out to be the rather bizarre privy. Figuring he couldn't get into too much trouble, he chose a direction.

The hallway was empty, though he heard people farther down. He couldn't move fast, given his injuries. He shuffled down the corridor and put his ear to the first door he came to. When he didn't hear anything, he tried the handle. The door opened.

This proved to be a guest room, done in such unusual and specific colours that one would assume it had been decorated with a particular guest in mind. It was done to look like what could only be called a night sky, with both stars and clouds. And in the middle of the gigantic bed were two of Necromis' servants, for whom the room had likely *not* been intended at all, fornicating as if their lives were about to end. Each had a brand on his shoulder of a bear, Necromis' symbol, and they looked healthy and well fed, as well as active. They were young, each perhaps no more than eighteen, and the lean one with long red hair was mounting the taller youth with brown hair with a power and lust that few wild horses could manage.

They had not noticed Lias.

He just stood for a moment, mouth open far more than the door. Eyes wide, he could only stare at the two of them. He'd never actually seen two men together. He'd heard stories, of course, but never had he witnessed it. It looked... painful. But the men—especially the one being penetrated—certainly did not seem like they were in pain. He knew he should leave just as quietly as he'd come, but his feet remained frozen in place. The slaves were loud enough that Lias wondered why no one had heard them.

The one with the long brown hair was responding in a manner that indicated, if anything, he wished his companion would go far, far deeper, clawing his back, then finally crying out loudly, his semen spurting onto his own belly. That was when the redhead growled, thrusting harder and deeper, finding his own pleasure. They bit and kissed and clawed as the redhead spent himself deep inside his lover, then collapsed, panting and laughing.

"You are right, my beauty," said the redhead, "it *is* more fun to do it in forbidden locations."

"Next, let us borrow Sir Necromis' shapeshifting pendant!" said the brown haired one. "We shall become stallions and take turns mounting each other."

Stifling a whimper, Lias backed out of the room, shutting the door. No. Just… *no*. He'd seen horses mate. It was not a pretty sight by any means. Eyes closed, he took a deep, calming breath. Maybe the next door would be far less… incendiary.

He continued down the hall, trying to put the images of the slaves out of his mind, albeit unsuccessfully. At the next door, he paused, hand on the latch. What would he find behind it? More rutting? One of those rites Necromis practiced? After steeling himself for the unknown, Lias cracked open the door and peered into the room.

Something fluttered — a *big* something. The room was done in golds, greens, and pinks, set up as if for the comfort of a creature rather than a person. A fire burned in a golden hearth, and before it was a great couch. Sunken into the floor was a pool of clear cold water, and the great windows were enchanted to show only a deep twilight over trees, not the hateful storm. There came a fluttering again, and then something appeared: a fragile, delicate, unspeakably lovely something, with skin and hair of purest gold, and crystal-clear butterfly wings. It blinked iridescent multi-faceted eyes at Lias, clad in breeches and boots, and sported an enormous pair of fluffy antennae on top of his head. Entranced, Lias couldn't look away.

"I-I'm sorry. I didn't mean to… intrude or anything." But he couldn't bring himself to actually leave the doorway. "What… are you, if I may ask? I've never seen another like you?"

"I'm a wizard," said the creature dryly. "Not a very good one. I changed like this for a party five months ago and can't change back. It was terribly humorous and charming then, but I'm rather tired of it."

"So… you're human? I'd offer to help, but I'm certainly no wizard. That said, is there anything I can do to help, non-magically?"

The creature sighed. "No. Not really. I'm afraid I'm stuck like this for another eight weeks yet, waiting for the Archer's Blood flower to bloom so I can make the antidote.

With my luck, it will be too cold, and the flower will not open, and I shall have to wait until next year." There came a loud thump from the next room. "My name is Khaylin. I think you met our randy young lovers next door. If they get caught, Necromis will not be pleased."

"I didn't exactly meet them, but, given what I witnessed, I agree that Necromis won't be too happy. I am Lias, by the way. It's a pleasure to meet you, Khaylin." It was also a pleasure to meet someone who didn't hate him on sight. For that, Lias was eternally grateful.

The lovers thumped and banged and giggled, then one screamed, "Oh, Micah, harder!"

Khaylin sighed. "Would you like to walk to the sitting room and have tea with me? I have a feeling they will not stop until one is pregnant."

"I'd love to." He followed Khaylin, utterly entranced by the man's appearance. "They're men. They can't actually get pregnant." He stopped and blinked at Khaylin. "Or can they? I've seen some… very interesting — if not outright bizarre — things, people included, since arriving here."

"Well, there *are* spells," said Khaylin. "I've seen them, but they are long and involved, very powerful, and take months to complete as well as an enormous amount of preparation beforehand. I sincerely doubt those two have done anything more than down a stamina potion. They certainly don't know any mages strong enough to cast that spell."

Lias shuddered. "I had…" He took a deep breath and closed his eyes for a moment. "…three daughters. I don't think I'd ever want to be pregnant, though." He smiled, a bit shakily, and sat down when Khaylin did.

Khaylin shrugged. "Is that because you think it makes you less of a man? I assisted my best friend's wife with her labour when he was ill and could not come near her, for fear of making her ill, too. I dare say there are knights who could not bear such suffering for so long. Lord Necromis has the spells in his library. He wished to use them with Sterling. Now they just sit and gather dust."

"Not less of a man," Lias explained. "I just recall the pain my wife went through, and that was more than enough. I remember wishing I could have done more to help her with the pain of childbirth, and I remember the awe I felt when she brought our children into this world." He sighed. "I'm sorry. I haven't really spoken to anyone since I've been here, so please forgive me if I say too much."

Khaylin seemed to study him, then asked "You're not, by chance, Lias the Nipper, Flinger of Poo?"

Lias groaned. So much for meeting someone who didn't know what he'd done. He sighed. "Yes. Though I'm not as angry now."

Khaylin laughed. "I have heard of all your antics from Merrigale. She is a dear friend. Yes, I must say you do seem more calm, though Necromis certainly did take the whip to you."

"Yes, he did. In retrospect, however, even his whip was kinder than the things I'd endured — or could endure — beyond these walls." Lias glanced at Khaylin. "Have you heard anything about him? All I've been told is that he's very sick, deathly ill."

Khaylin nodded. "He took several bites, and they are known for inflicting disease. If Necromis does not die or become the walking undead, he will be very lucky indeed."

Lias sank into the chair. "It's my fault."

"Don't be silly, you didn't send Necromis out there."

"No," Lias said. "But the first time he fought the calf, it was because I'd shouted for help when the thing came after me in Necromis' chambers. The next day or so after, Necromis went out to fight it again. It's when he brought me this." Lias held up the pendant hanging around his neck.

"You could do worse than to love him," said Khaylin. "But I suspect you have been told that."

Lias looked at Khaylin. "You're the second one who's said that, but no one will talk to me long enough to explain. I know Necromis still mourns Sterling. Why would how I feel make any difference? Necromis despises me."

91

Khaylin chuckled briefly. "Perhaps a little right now. I will explain to you all I can. I do know Necromis rather well."

"I've tried to change, at least enough that he won't send me away or kill me," Lias said. "I spent far too long enduring more than I care to recount before he came along. It left me angry—at everyone and everything. I lashed out at him, undeservedly so, I will admit. But... I don't know what to do anymore. I'm rather stunned you don't hate me as well since you know what I've done."

Khaylin shrugged. "I used to hate them all, but at last I came to understand it is Necromis' choice. He is tormented by Sterling's death. We who call him friend only want to see him happy. But why he picks the angriest, most... well, I will not insult you. That is not my intention. I wonder only what draws him to the most broken slaves."

"So do I," Lias muttered. "I still don't know why my feelings about him make any difference, especially to him."

"I have wondered that myself. Not you, specifically but..." Khaylin leaned close, speaking in a confidential tone. "I wonder if there is not a curse. I am a new mage with little experience, but I *am* a mage. This speaks to me of curse-breaking."

One eyebrow raised, Lias stared at Khaylin. "Curse-breaking? Wouldn't bringing someone like me here be more like curse-making?"

Khaylin shook his head, making his feelers wave. "Curses are funny things, and the rules for breaking them are very specific, tailored to each curse. To win the romantic love of a man who despises you could be a curse-breaker."

Lias' jaw dropped open. "*Romantic... love?*" he squeaked. "I... uh... I'm not... I don't like men like Necromis does."

Khaylin shrugged. "Well, I suspect that is where the curse-breaking comes into play. Clearly, it would take a great deal of strength and heart for you to go from loathing him to willingly giving him your body. Especially after all you have been through. Curses must be broken with an act

92

of profound power. Such a love would be profound enough to send Bonecracker back to the abyss."

"I don't loathe him," Lias protested. "Not really. I hated him when I first got here, but circumstances have shown me that I'm far safer here than anywhere else. But if he's indeed trying to break a curse, why has it not worked before now? From what I've heard, he's had many slaves like me. Well, of a sort, anyway."

"They did not love him, not that way. He sent some of them to the hunting lodge, and you saw two more of his little pets just now breaking his furniture. And though they are no doubt profoundly grateful, they did not love him. He seeks love of a very specific kind. I can think only that he is trying to rid himself of a curse."

"I suppose there are worse things," Lias said. "Though I can't think what sort of curse he'd be under that would warrant such a method to break."

"Nor can I. But let us get you back to your room. I cannot imagine your absence has not been noticed."

"I want to thank you," Lias said as they left the room and started down the hall. "No one else has taken any sort of time to talk to me."

"Could it possibly have anything to do with the biting and the poo-flinging?" asked Khaylin with mock innocence.

Lias managed a chuckle. "I know not of what you speak," he said as they stopped at his door.

Lias was about to enter his room when, on the floor below, some soldiers dragged in a tall man who was fighting them with all his strength. There was shouting and some punches thrown, then the man was forced to his knees. Lias and Khaylin watched as Necromis appeared, weak, sickly, and moving very slowly. He was wrapped in a heavy robe, his long white hair dull and tangled, his eyes glassy. The soldiers saluted their master as Lias drew back slightly, wishing to watch without being noticed.

"We've captured the pirate," said one.

Necromis stared at the prisoner, then said softly, "Samuel?"

The pirate hung his head and seemed ashamed. "Aye, my lord."

Necromis stepped closer. "Samuel, why are you here? Did I not send you to the hunting lodge?"

"You did, my lord, but... I was not happy."

"Then why did you not write to me? Why did you not let me know? Samuel... you must know the penalty for piracy!"

"I do my lord, but..."

"It is your nature," said Necromis sadly. "It is what your heart demands. And the law of the land demands your blood."

"I am sorry, Necromis. I know I shall hang, and I bear you no grudge."

"No," said Necromis quietly. "You shall not hang. I shall not permit it. Perhaps another shall see you come to that end, but it shall not be by my hands. I have need of a privateer. Would you agree to serve me?"

"Yes!" said Samuel. "I would and gladly!"

"Then I shall have the contracts drawn up, and you will serve me."

"For what am I seeking?" asked Samuel as the soldiers removed his chains.

"A trader's ship, one bold enough to risk the southern inlet and take slaves."

Samuel rubbed his abraded wrists. "There are few that desperate. I can think of only two. They will not be hard to track down. Are you searching for anyone specifically?"

"They captured my current slave Lias."

"Oh, I've heard of your dainty fair boy."

"Samuel..." said Necromis wearily.

"Apologies."

Lias curled a lip, while Khaylin smothered a laugh. Necromis continued to speak.

"They captured his wife Merdine. He would like to know of her fate."

"Then I shall do my best to ensure he learns it."
Samuel gazed at Necromis, then, after a few moments, said,
"How can I thank you for my life?"

Necromis shrugged. He looked beaten and sad, even
tearful. Finally, he spoke. "A kiss?"

"For my life, I shall give you a kiss. I am sorry it was
never anything more."

Lias watched Samuel kiss Necromis. It was soft and
loving, filled with the implication of a hard road walked.
Eventually, it ended, and Samuel departed to find his crew
and ship. Necromis allowed himself to be led back to his
room, while Lias processed what he had just heard and seen.

The tale was true. There was a hunting lodge. The
slaves were not being murdered. Slowly, thinking on the
interaction between Necromis and Samuel, Lias entered his
room.

Necromis meant to search for Merdine. He had
hired a privateer to do just that, without informing Lias. Not
for show. Not to win favour. But to find a wife for the slave
who had scarred his face. Lias closed his eyes, wondering
how he could have been so wrong about the man.

When he opened his eyes, he saw Hawthorne gazing
at him irritably.

"Lias, you have two choices: you can stay in bed and
heal, or I can rip your stitches out with a fork."

Lias grimaced. "I apologize. I just..." He gestured
helplessly toward the door where Khaylin stood. "I needed
to move." He sat down gingerly, the walk having taken
more out of him than he'd realized. "I won't do it again."

"Lias, I have a toddler who behaves better than you
do. And that is a very sad commentary on you as an adult."

Lias gave Khaylin a defeated smile. "Thank you
again, Khaylin." He laid down, face to the wall. It was a
pleasant diversion while it lasted.

A small rat stood on his pillow to look at him. It was
rather an odd thing to notice that even Necromis' rats were
shiny and healthy. Khaylin departed for his own room,
while Hawthorne seated himself on the floor to check his

patient. He tried to shoo the rat, but it just stared at him, as though the concept of fearing humans never entered its brain.

Despite the twinge of depression creeping up, Lias couldn't help but smile at the rat. He reached out, putting his hand close to see what the creature did. If he got bit... Well, he'd certainly had worse wounds. The rat, however, seemed affronted by the gesture and galloped clumsily away. Hawthorne carefully looked Lias over, checking injuries.

"You must be very worried right now, pondering your fate should Necromis die."

Lias remained silent for a moment. He could say what Hawthorne expected him to say, that he cared only for his own hide should Necromis die. Or he could be honest. Not that Hawthorne would believe him anyway. "I'm more concerned about him."

Hawthorne did not look terribly impressed, nor as if he much believed him. "You will become my responsibility should he die. Though what I shall do with you, I cannot say."

Lias shrugged. Did it really matter? Meeting Khaylin, speaking with someone who didn't hate him, had been the best thing to happen to him in a long time. But it had been temporary. "Do what you will with me," Lias said, glancing at Hawthorne for a moment. "I am a prisoner and a slave."

And lonely, though he had no intention of voicing such things to anyone.

"I suppose my wife could use you to bite lace-holes in the corsets she loves to make."

That surprised a laugh out of Lias, but he attempted to stifle it. He didn't dislike Hawthorne. In fact, he actually had a grudging respect for the man, though he honestly didn't know why. Should something happen to Necromis, Lias figured he'd better off with Hawthorne than anyone else.

"Whatever you see fit to do with me."

96

"And escape the first chance you get, I suppose. Well, I'd foil all your plans and let you go."

Lias sighed. "I haven't tried to escape, except the confines of this single room, in a while."

"And the fact that you could barely walk has nothing to do with that. Hold your breath." Hawthorne swiped something very cold and tingly down his back.

Lias hissed and tensed up. "Nothing, actually," he grumbled through gritted teeth. "I just needed to explore beyond this room. I came back. Did I not?"

"Lias, it will take far more than one day of good behaviour to convince me you are redeemed. I saw the bite you put on that Seven Isles slave. Bonecracker haunts your soul. I will not be unkind to you, but I will not trust you. Not for a while." He carefully applied the ointment to the breaks in the skin, then bandaged the injuries.

"You will never be convinced," Lias said. He shrugged. "I can't change that. At this point, I can only try my best to change myself."

"Then I shall fetch you a diaper so you may do so."

The door opened, and a slave crept in, none other than the tall youth with the long brown hair Lias had witnessed being willingly and joyously rutted by his lover. "Sir Hawthorne, I was told to find you and inform you that your wife and child have come to join you in the castle until such time as it is safe to return."

Hawthorne simply raised an eyebrow. "I'm surprised you could get out from under Micah long enough to do so."

"Yes, well, a sword such as his is meant to be enjoyed."

Lias bit his tongue. He'd seen far more of the slave than most... perhaps other than Micah... had.

"You have a child?" Lias asked Hawthorne. He could see how the man would be a good father, though the thought of a child reminded him of his own girls. He swallowed back the heartache.

"One. A monster of a little girl. I've decided to simply despair of her being a proper lady now and bought her a pony, set of armor, and a sword." He looked to the youth. "Though no doubt it does not compare to Micah's."

"Treasure her," Lias murmured. He turned away and took a deep breath. He needed to think about something else. Anything else.

"I'd invite you to try his skill, but I would rather not share," said the youth.

"That is fine," said Hawthorne. "Necromis made me swear that if ever such an urge overcame me, his sword would be the one I fell upon, or he upon mine. Alas, I fear it will long remain sheathed."

"I assume Necromis prefers to… give, rather than receive, in such instances," said Lias.

The slave bit his lip hard and said *nothing*. Hawthorne, however, was a friend and a fellow knight, and therefore was not obliged to keep secrets.

"Well, let's just say that one night I entered his room to find him giving as well as receiving three guests. I should have been shocked, but I found myself rather admiring his skill."

Lias blinked. "Three? How can one man…" Then it dawned on him just how a single person—even a man—could, indeed, 'entertain' more than one person at a single time. "Oh."

Hawthorne looked to the brown-haired youth. "Dava, go get a room ready for my wife and daughter and see there is food waiting when they arrive. I shall have to work a little longer on Poo-Bite's injuries."

Lias groaned. "Great," he muttered. *Why* did he have to throw his chamber pot? Why couldn't he have… kicked or thrown something else, something more… savoury, at least? "I'm never going to live that down."

"Not as long as I am alive," Hawthorne assured him. "And you're lucky to *be* alive. And now I am going to be utterly heartless and make you eat something. You're nothing but bones. Tell me true: when was your last full meal?"

Lias opened his mouth to answer, then shut it. "I don't remember," he murmured. "I don't think I've had one since my initial capture."

"And you've not really been well enough since you came here to hold down more than a few bites. I'll see you get one. Lias, I do not know if you fully understand this, but you are dying. You're thin to the point of being cadaverous, there is not a spot on you that is not bruised, cut, or septic, and if you do not rest, then all my efforts are for naught. I may as well give you the potion I use to put old horses out of their misery."

"But I do not feel so ill now," said Lias, taking care to ensure his tone was submissive, not confrontational. He did not wish for Hawthorne to think he was arguing against him.

"Do you not?" Hawthorne seemed surprised. "Because you look terrible."

"I did not say I felt well. But good enough to be restless. I really did only wish to look around."

"And not to escape or harm yourself?"

"At one point, I wanted to die. I had nothing left, no reason to remain alive." Things had changed, though he couldn't pinpoint when... or what, exactly. "I am sorry that I've not followed your instructions. I will do so from now on. I know no one here cares whether I die or not, but I'm no longer ready for death."

"*That is not true!*" snapped Hawthorne. "That is *not* true, and you will stop saying it now!"

Lias flinched, eyes going wide. "I..." Who on earth even remotely gave a damn? "I apologize, though I honestly don't have any idea who does care. But if it means that much, then I will not repeat it."

"Necromis cares. You may find that hard to believe, but he does. He lost someone that meant more to him than he can ever explain. I can only imagine what it would be like to lose my wife, and, frankly, I don't want to. He tries to seal

99

the hole in his heart by helping slaves who are also being slowly murdered by uncaring men. How would you respond to such a loss?"

"My first wife died from an illness with no name. My second wife was abducted," Lias said. "I'm a slave because I swore to find her, no matter the costs. I left my daughters with a friend, and now I know I will never see them again. So, yes, I know what it's like to lose someone I love more than life itself. I've done it. Twice."

Hawthorne's demeanour softened visibly. "I am sorry for your loss. Truly, I am. But hate will not find your lady again."

Lias stared at Hawthorne for a moment. It was the first anyone had said such a thing, but, more than that, it was the nicest thing Hawthorne had ever uttered to him. "Thank you."

There was silence, perhaps a slightly uncomfortable one. Then a huge black and white nose poked into the room, snuffling. Hawthorne rolled his eyes. The eyeroll became a noise of pure aggravation when a little girl shouted, "Why can't my horsie come into the house, Mummy?"

Lias chuckled. "Your little one, I take it?"

"Yes, and thanks to the whims of a dear friend afflicted by just the smallest touch of madness, I shall now have ponies in my bed."

Lias snorted and rolled his eyes. "Can't be any worse than Rufus. I honestly don't see how Necromis can sleep with such bed-hogging beast."

"If you'd seen his last lover, you'd not ask such a thing," muttered Hawthorne before he slipped away to greet his wife and child.

Lias wasn't sure he wanted to know. He settled on the bed and closed his eyes, fully intending on taking a nap. But he couldn't get the talk with Hawthorne out of his head no matter how hard he tried. Did Necromis really care? Or was the man only trying to heal a broken slave out of guilt and compulsion? Lias didn't know what to think. He

100

certainly hadn't done anything to warrant the man's care, especially after the things he'd said and done.

But then, there *was* the conversation with Samuel…

"I was wrong," Lias said, draping one arm over his eyes. "But I have no idea how to fix it. Or if it can ever be fixed."

Chapter Seven

More weeks passed. Life settled into a quiet routine. Necromis remained ill but was recovering, at least from the rumours Lias heard. He found he himself had become something of a side-show attraction, the Wild Dog of Forest Keep. Once Lias even woke up to find the king himself, as well as a few attendants, standing over him.

"Bloody ugly," was the verdict. Then they left.

Several days after that charming incident, Merrigale came into Lias' room, looking harried and tired.

"How would you like to go for a cart ride? I know you are still weak, but all you have to do is come into town and sit while I get a few things. I've no one else to go with, and if the horse is alone, she decides to walk home without me."

Lias welcomed the chance to get out, even though he figured he'd be just as much a spectacle in town. Still... oh, to see outside again!

"I can go with you and make sure she doesn't get wanderlust," he agreed.

"And you'll behave."

"I swear on my glowing reputation."

He carefully got up and dressed in a shirt and thin pants. Merrigale helped him, urging him to be careful as he was still weak. Finally, she helped him into a pair of socks and shoes.

Much of Lias' existence and mental state, as well as his physical one, had improved. He was still lonely, but Khaylin was a regular visitor. However, he had not been around for a few days — off looking for the proper herbs to become a man again, no doubt. And he and Hawthorne had come to a sort of friendship as well, or at the very least, they no longer disliked each other. Merrigale, too, had warmed a little towards him, and she now took Lias' arm and slowly walked him out of his room, down the sweeping golden staircase to the lower levels, and out the door to where a disgruntled red bay mare was making faces at her handler.

"She's spirited. No wonder she gets wanderlust!" said the groom.

Lias slowly and carefully climbed into the cart, then looked to the groom. "What is her name?"

"Scarlett. She was meant to be a fine hunter, but she won't have a soul on her back for a moment! She doesn't mind the harness and the cart, and she's a lamb with a sulky, but no one sits on her back. She won't have it. But she has to work for her keep, and since she tolerates the carts well and prefers the long outings, we let her work on her own terms. But what a hunter she would have been!"

"She's beautiful," Lias said as Merrigale got into the driver's seat and took the reins. They started down the dirt road. "Very well built and strong. How long have you had her?"

"She was born on the grounds," replied Merrigale. "Her sire and dam are two of the finest in our stable, but both with heads of concrete. Not mean, but definitely animals with very firmly set opinions. Here, look to the right, now, and see Sterling, the master's favourite and named for his lost love."

The horse was an astonishingly brilliant, nearly metallic, silver-grey colour, with white socks, mane, tail, and nose. As they drove, the horse followed the mare along the road from within his pasture, head and tail held high. His shoes appeared to be crafted of silver, and when he tossed his head, his eyes were an eerie pale gold. He kept pace effortlessly, the sun showing faint tiger-stripe patterns on his shoulders.

"A gift from the elven queen who holds reign to the west. You will not see another like him in your life," said Merrigale.

The stallion's eyes held far more intelligence than Lias had ever seen in any animal. Lias wondered if maybe it was due to the horse's previous owner. He'd heard tales of elven horses and their superior intelligence to other horses.

"Magnificent," Lias murmured. "If he is Necromis' favorite, why does Necromis not ride him?"

103

"Necromis says he cheats at chess." Merrigale pondered that. "I'm afraid to ask him what that means."

Lias laughed. "Given what I've seen of Rufus, I'd take Necromis at his word on that."

After a little over an hour's drive, the town loomed ahead behind a protective wooden palisade. Lias saw no guards, but he figured they were there somewhere. Farms dotted the countryside outside the walls, and a few people stopped what they were doing to watch the cart go by. Lias hoped they were merely curious and that they had no idea what sort of behavior he was really known for within the castle. Though, given that the king even knew, Lias didn't hold much hope.

Merrigale pulled up to a large building within the market district, handing Lias the reins. "Now just sit and enjoy the sunshine. That's all you need do. Since you are dressed in slave garb, some may come to look at you and see if you are worth making an offer on. Most folk are polite, but you *are* your master's property, and that means if anyone tries to handle you, you're free to bite. *That* should please you."

Taking the reins, Lias nodded. He watched Merrigale disappear into the building, then he looked around the market. The outdoor stalls bustled with people, primarily women with children in tow. Lias watched the little families and shoved his sorrow to the farthest reaches of his mind. He'd left his girls with someone he trusted. He knew he'd never see them again, but at least they were safe.

Most of the people seemed to be peasants, though a few nobles mingled as well. Lias hadn't expected to see nobles. Such people usually sent servants to fetch various goods in the market. After a while, Lias became aware of a few men clustered nearby. They were staring at him as if appraising. Lias rolled his shoulders, nerves bristling. He prayed Merrigale hurried. While he had little desire to resort to his biting tactic, he'd do it if anyone dared lay a finger on him.

One young man, sporting the outlandish garb of a fop, approached and peered into the wagon at him. He wrinkled his nose, then, quite without Lias' permission, dribbled some perfume on him—very costly perfume that smelled of sunlight on hyacinth.

"You there—Lump. What manner of slave are you? My companions and I were just wondering what use you could possibly be."

Wrinkling his nose, Lias glared and snarled at the man. "I've eaten things prettier than you." He snapped his teeth for emphasis.

The fop was not daunted in the least. He dripped a couple more drops of perfume on Lias. "I should think you have, but that was not what I asked you. What use are you, or are you truly only ballast?"

A second man came over, still a fop but with better manners. "Do leave the poor beast alone, would you? I'm sure he's not just ballast." The man raised a hand and said quietly, "I'm just going to look at that mark on your shoulder, don't be afraid. There's a grand fellow."

Lias tensed. "Unless you are a healer, do *not* touch me," he growled low.

"Oh, don't be a fuss, I'm just looking." The man clearly knew how to behave like a healer because he did manage to get his look at the scar, though he definitely respected the waves of hostility Lias was emitting. "There's a fine fellow," he said softly.

What the man wished to see, he never did say. Perhaps he was simply horrified Lias had been so deeply scarred. He certainly knew better than to push his luck and withdrew his hand. Then the perfume-dribbler decided he needed to see what his companion had looked at.

"What's so fascinating?" he asked and tugged at the fabric sharply.

Something snapped in Lias. Within a split second, his teeth sank deep into the perfumed idiot's hand. Lias shook it like a rabid dog, snarling and growling. The fop shrieked and screamed and struggled, the entire spectacle drawing a crowd. Lias didn't care. He jerked away, blood dripping from his mouth.

The man who had looked at Lias' shoulder seemed more concerned for Lias, oddly enough. Somehow, he was suddenly in the cart and… touching him. Lias should have wanted to kill him… but he didn't. This man was not here to hurt him. He almost heard the words in his head. It was disconcerting and a bit frightening and clearly the work of some sort of magic, but this man did not wish to hurt him. Then he was being gently held, a soft song playing in his head. He was safe. He was okay. He was loved. No one was going to hurt him…

Lias began to shake. Uncontrollably. The market, the crowd that had gathered at the commotion. It all faded. He squeezed his eyes shut. He had no idea who this man was, or what the man did. Lias' heart pounded, and he swore it would burst. No one had ever touched him like this man did, like Lias actually mattered, like someone actually cared.

"There's a grand fellow. It's all right. There we go. You just lie down and rest. Do not trouble yourself with fools. Here, this will make you feel better…"

Lias felt the tiniest pinprick on his shoulder. The world became a quiet and peaceful place.

"It bit me!" shrieked the fop.

"And whose fault is that?" snapped the man holding Lias. "By all that the White Bear guards, you're not only the most foolish man I ever met, but the most badly dressed. Take thee to a tailor."

The man gasped roughly, as if he had never heard such an insult.

Lias watched, his brain fuzzy but clear enough to see the outright shock on the fop's face. He wanted to laugh. He couldn't get a sound out, though. Rage and hatred had taken hold the second the idiot had touched him, but now it began to fade away. Lias struggled to cling to it. His rage, his hatred—they had been the only things he had, his only defenses against the world. The man who held him threatened that security, yet Lias couldn't dredge up the slightest bit of either emotion toward him.

The man holding Lias managed to convince him to lie down in the cart, then hopped out to look to his friend. "Yes, he certainly tagged you, didn't he?"

"And you didn't care at all!" wailed his companion. "And you a mage sworn to the healing arts! You use your tricks on a slave that mauled me and then call me badly dressed!"

"I do care. But you have to stop doing foolish things. Stand near the fountain. We will get you cleaned up and pretty again." After a moment, the man added, "Then we'll take you to a tailor."

The man turned back to Lias again, stroking him, using some sort of magic to calm him. Lias tried to growl. He did not like this magic at all. It would be too easy to use against someone, to make them to submit to things they may not care for. With Herculean effort, Lias managed a huff, and the man laughed.

"I'm not here to hurt you. You rest now. The sun is warm, and you are safe." He paused and seemed to be pondering something. "Do you, by chance, belong to Necromis?"

Lias sighed. Yeah, apparently, the biting thing was gonna haunt him. "Yes," he breathed.

"Tell me, how does he fare? There is word that he is gravely ill."

Lias had no idea how, or even if, he should answer that. He managed a faint growl. The man gave him a friendly pat, then left to attend to his friend.

It was like the night Necromis forced him to eat the lichen. He was warm and safe, and all was well with the world. Except not quite. He wished they had found Merdine by now, but he had been healing and Necromis had been ill so long. Was she well? Was she, like he, enjoying the sun? Was she at least safe, as he was? He hoped she was safe and not pregnant by some disgusting, lecherous monster. Then, somewhere outside of the little shell of peace and quiet the healing mage had wrought, Lias was dead certain he heard the voice of his daughter Sunni, calling faintly from across the square.

"Stepmother, come quick! They have sweets for sale!"

Ice shot up Lias' spine, and he gave himself a shake, scattering the warm sleepy feeling off of himself like leaves in a fall wind. There was no mistaking that sweet voice, but had it only been part of his dream? He sat up and looked around, a little befuddled. He was certain he had heard Sunni, but was Sunni there to speak?

Then, across the square, a wealthy lady in a spectacular grey gown followed by a slave bearing her parcels moved aside. Lias' jaw dropped at what he saw. The world around him dissolved as he watched his family — *his* family — walk along the stalls. Happy. They looked... happy. His baby girls. His wife. The ones he'd fought for, the ones he'd lived for. They moved along, completely oblivious to him. He wanted to shout at them, scream his daughters' names. But he was still too sedated. His heart ached with every step they took as they moved farther away. From him.

Then... as his children and his wife... *his* wife! The woman for whom he had been raped, chained, beaten, sold, and finally ended up in a cart as a guardian for a horse with wanderlust! Then as his wife gently shooed the children out of the market, they were met by...

Broadin.

Lias tightened his fists as rage and heartache filled every ounce of his being. His world turned red. He grabbed the edge of the wagon, ready to jump out and kill the bastard who'd stolen his family. Injuries or no injuries, he would...

But he stopped. Every move hurt and still left him in agony some nights. And then he remembered his status. No one would think twice about putting a slave to death for attacking a man. Could he even attack with the herbs still dulling his senses?

Instead of leaving the wagon, Lias watched as the happy family walked out of sight. Nausea rose, threatening what remained of Lias' last meal. He fought it back.

Everything he'd fought for, everything he'd endured… It had all been for absolutely nothing.

Then… everything became very quiet. The healer with the foppish fashion sense was beside him, and there was a tiny thorn-like pricking sensation in his neck. It had to be a potion made of that strange moss because then there were flowers and birds and peaceful things. Had he had some sort of a rage fit? There were people all around him, and Merrigale and the man were talking. The wagon was loaded, and the foppish man stayed by his side as they drove back to the castle, speaking gently to him. Had he been screaming? He thought maybe he had, but it was so hard to tell.

Lias tried to speak, but nothing came out. He blinked slowly and watched the countryside go by like a dream. What had happened? He'd been sitting in the wagon. He'd bitten another man's hand. He'd been touched by the healer. Then he'd…

Visions flashed through Lias' mind.

His daughters. His wife.

Broadin.

Lias moaned and closed his eyes, the nausea returning. He'd been played a fool. He'd been through every torment, every nightmare, only to find it had all been a cruel, sick ruse.

He was carried into the castle, but not to his solitary room. He was carried into Necromis' chamber and placed on a rather lavish daybed near the fire. He was shaky and confused, and it took some time to recognize the badly-wasted man on the main bed as Necromis. The knight was sickly and skeletal, and his glorious white mane was lank and dirty. He looked more like a cadaver than lord of a keep, and when he spoke, his voice was a paper-thin whisper.

"Great bear above, Lias, who did you bite this time?"

109

The mage had apparently followed Lias to the castle because he began seeing to Necromis, whispering as Hawthorne approached the healer. Apparently, there was little the mage could do to improve upon Hawthorne's care, and he departed after being warned to speak to no one about how bad Necromis' condition truly was. Then Hawthorne turned to Lias.

"And what have you been up to, you rogue?"

The room spun when Lias tried to get up. He sank back down. "I... I saw... them," he muttered. "My babies. My... wife."

"Here... come here and tell me." It was Necromis' voice, but so weak, it was like a whisper from a grave. "I can hardly hear you from over there. Come talk to me. Where did you see your babies?"

With Hawthorne's help, Lias managed to get up and make his way to the bed, stumbling, not thinking about where he was going or what he was doing. At Necromis' bidding, he lay down beside the man. Then he pressed into Necromis' side, face buried against him. He just needed solace and cared not from whence it came. Just some basic human comfort.

"The market," Lias murmured. He swallowed as a lump of emotion began forming in his throat. His heart ached more than he ever thought possible. He squeezed his eyes shut, but not quick enough to stop a tear from dripping onto Necromis' arm. "My babies. She made it all happen. I would have died for her. But she and Broadin..."

Hawthorne gasped quietly as he grasped the implication of Lias' words. Necromis weakly folded Lias into an embrace, kissing his brow.

"My poor dear Lias. How we misjudged you. If anyone had a right to bite, it was you. But why would she do so cruel a thing? And are you certain she did? Is it not possible that Broadin's finding her was an accident?"

Lias shook his head, unable to speak. Everything he'd had with her had been a lie. Every sweet word of love. Every touch. Every kiss. She'd captured his heart, then shattered it into a thousand pieces. He couldn't bring himself to care what happened anymore. The one reason he'd fought to live this long had betrayed him like no one else ever could. He gasped, finding his voice.

"No, it makes sense now, I see how the game was played," said Lias. "My first wife, my love, Elyssa, was a lady. That made our daughters nobility as well. Daughters with such a lineage command a great bride-price, but Elyssa and I swore our daughters would marry for love, as she did. They would be free to choose, and if it was but a fisherman, so be it. I remember now Merdine trying to talk me out of this, saying we could use the money, but what is gold? It is not worth a little girl's heart. So she found a way to get my children all to herself…"

Lias broke, weeping so hard, it was as if everything within himself had been broken. He scarcely felt Necromis stroke his hair.

"There, there, my pretty one," whispered Necromis. "There, there. Necromis shall make this right, though I am not certain how."

Necromis reached up a thin, white, and skeletal hand to tug a bell-rope, and within moments Hawthorne was joined by Sir Thordin and Lady Solecil. Necromis explained in a quiet voice what had happened and where the betrayers had last been seen. The knights departed quickly.

"They shall not get far. I doubt they realize they have fled into the jaws of the bear. I swear to you, Lias, you will see your babies ere the sun sets tomorrow."

Lias lifted his head to look at Necromis, really *look* at the man. For the first time since meeting Necromis, Lias saw kindness—and caring—in the man's eyes. "I've done nothing but bring you trouble. Why would you do this for me? I've not deserved it."

"And you did deserve to have your wife betray you to traders?" Necromis swallowed painfully. "I've seen kings commit worse crimes for less. I long suspected the game played upon you but did not voice my thoughts without proof. I have now my proof. You were betrayed for the most base of reasons. I say you deserve a dose of kindness. And, dare I say, revenge."

Lias' head swam. He closed his eyes and rested his head on Necromis' chest again. "Thank you," he murmured. "I…" He shook his head where it lay. "I don't know how I could ever repay you for such a thing." He thought about the pirate, Samuel, and smiled. "A kiss?"

"Oh, you saw that, did you? Naughty thing."

Necromis carefully tipped Lias' head back, looking into his eyes as if searching for something. Then he moved his head closer and gave him the very softest and most gentle of kisses. When it was over, Necromis said quietly, "I ask only that you grant me one small favour. That you look into your heart and ask if perhaps, just… perhaps… you could love me. Nothing more. That will be thanks enough."

Lias blinked slowly. His brain was fuzzy again, but not as it had been before. Something had changed. He didn't know what. Or when. His lips tingled, and he swore he still felt Necromis on them. Had such a thing happened before this moment, he would have been repulsed. But he wasn't. He realized he cared about Necromis. But could he ever love the man like Necromis wanted him to? Lias started to say he couldn't… but he stopped before the words made it out. A part of him—a tiny part—wasn't so sure anymore.

"I…" He swallowed. The air felt thick between them. "I will do as you ask," he said finally. "I can tell you this: I do care for you, Necromis."

"And do you at last believe I care about you as well?"

"I do," Lias answered. "I am sorry, too. Sorry for the hell I have put you through since my arrival."

"Oh, in that case, I get another kiss." This one was light and playful. Necromis was pushing his luck, but not in a manner that would upset his new friend. "Will you stay beside me tonight?"

Lias found something within himself. A small piece of sunlight and hope. It was very tiny, and if Necromis could not bring him his daughters, then it would likely die, but for now… he felt a little lighter.

"Tell you what," said Lias softly. "I'll run, and if you can catch me, I'll stay."

"Fine. I shall have the groom saddle my fastest snail." Necromis closed his eyes and sighed. "What a pair we are — well matched in strength and health."

"But we'll mend," said Lias softly.

"Shall we? There are days I wonder."

Necromis closed his eyes. Lias pressed a soft kiss to Necromis' lips. When Lias drew back, he found Necromis gazing at him.

"Go to sleep," he said, sounding somewhere between amused and annoyed.

Necromis fell into a light doze. Lias was no less tired, but he found he was not quite ready for sleep yet. He carefully slipped out of bed and limped to the window, gazing at the sun setting behind the endless plume of smoke that was Bonecracker's temple. On the road far below, grey shadows that once were people walked silently, men who had once been knights but were now empty shades without purpose. They chanted as they walked, their voices eerily beautiful, yet also frightening when one considered they were dead.

"The knights are here because the evil is here," Lias whispered to himself. Why had that once seemed so hard to believe?

His attention was drawn by Necromis swearing softly. Slowly, painfully, the knight sat up, looking like a vision of death. He carefully climbed out of bed, appearing as if a breath might knock him down.

"Going for a pub crawl, don't wait up."

Lias watched him depart, remembering the knight had rites to which he must attend. Being gravely ill was, apparently, not an excuse to miss them. He almost followed out of curiosity but then shook his head. It was none of his business, and he was tired of being his own worst enemy.

Instead, he watched the procession of the dead, wondering what his own fate would be when he passed.

After a short while, Lias went back to bed, paying no heed to Merrigale as she came to set up the bath for Necromis.

* * *

Necromis was back in less than an hour, demurely wrapped in a brocade robe, sporting a few streaks and smudges of blood. He looked weak and seemed cowed, as if he had done something to earn the displeasure of the being to which he had prayed. He slipped into the waiting bath, then gave Lias a small smile.

"Come join me?"

Lias smiled but did not move. "Your rites... Do they involve inflicting wounds on yourself? Your robe has blood on it."

"They do involve the sacrifice of... certain creatures. Tonight, though, my sacrifice was met with displeasure. I had hoped for a small return of health, but instead, I am weaker than ever I was. I have questions that require answers, and there are times I wonder if ever I shall be well again."

"I think you will be. I have to believe that."

Necromis gazed at him steadily. "I hope so. Would you... care to join me? No obligation. It would just be nice."

"No repercussions should I say no?"

"Not one. Save denying yourself the pleasure that is hot water."

Lias smiled. "I am conflicted! I'm not certain if... oh, to the demons with it, hot water does sound nice."

Lias came to join Necromis, stepping into the glorious warmth that was a deep hot bath. Oh, he had missed these. When had he last just slipped into a tub full of hot water? Truly, he could fall asleep. The tub was so large and deep. Easily with room enough for two and a pan of coals beneath to keep the water hot for a long time. The pair fell into peaceful silence, half asleep, enjoying the soothing warmth...

114

That was when the door flew open, and Lias' three little girls thundered into the room. They were young and excited enough that they did not question why Daddy was naked in the tub with another man. Sunni, in fact, was so delighted to see her Daddy again that she gleefully threw herself into the bath to hug him.

"Hi!" she said to Necromis, whose expression implied the child's foot had gone someplace it oughtn't.

Shock held Lias frozen for a split second. Then he threw his arms around his daughters, all three of them at once, and didn't bother to stop the tears. He kissed their heads and held them tight.

"My babies," he whispered through the tears. "Oh, Necromis. You have no idea how much I love you for this. I never thought I'd see them again."

"The pleasure is mine," he said softly. "Along with a small helping of mortification."

Lias laughed. "I don't think I could ever tell you how much this means to me." He looked into Necromis' eyes for a moment. "Or what you have come to mean to me…"

"Daddy, why are you and your friend both in the same bath? Don't you have more than one? I hate sharing baths. Where did you go, Daddy? Stepmother said you didn't love us anymore, we were too naughty!"

Lias knew those questions would come up, but he took his kiss first before answering. "It's a long story, Sunni. I have never stopped loving any of you. I… got lost." He glanced up at Necromis and smiled. "But Necromis found me."

"I like his hair! I want hair like that when I grow up!" Sunni shouted as her father moved her out of the bath. "Why are you so pretty? Are you magic?"

"Better," said Necromis. "I am a knight of the Order of the White Bear."

Necromis suddenly had the attention of all three children.

115

Then the eldest of the trio, Elderwyn, made her opinion of this known rather loudly. "Daddy made friends with a knight!"

All three began screeching and jumping like they were insane. Necromis seemed as if he wished his newly-acquired children were mute.

Lias winced. He gave Necromis an apologetic grin. "Did I mention they were loud?" He tried to calm the girls down, moving one hand in a shushing motion. "We are friends, yes."

Elderwyn was the eldest and, therefore, the most likely to make assumptions. "Well, you're naked in a bath with him. Are you going to get married?"

"What? I... no!"

Elderwyn seemed crestfallen, and she pouted, arms crossed. "Why not?"

"Uh... I... well..." Lias glanced at Necromis and mouthed, 'help.'

Necromis gave him a wicked, wicked smile, green eyes nearly luminous with mischief. "Well, that would be because he wanted to tell the three of you first, so you could help with the wedding preparations."

It was a *very* good thing Lias was sitting. His jaw dropped open, and his eyes went wide. "Wait. *What?*"

"Well, Lias, my love, surely, these three adorable children need two parents, and one with the proper background to teach them to be ladies. We discussed all this, don't you remember?" The look on Necromis' face suggested he knew he was in for a spanking but too frail to actually get one.

Lias blinked, struck speechless for a moment. Then his eyes narrowed. He leaned close to Necromis' ear, whispering, "You're damn lucky I'm in no position to kick your ass."

"And I am in no condition to be kicked." Necromis kissed his nose. "The proposal is real. You are not obligated to accept," he whispered in return.

116

Nothing could have prepared Lias for that. He stared at Necromis, barely aware of the girls chattering to each other nearby. "You're serious, aren't you?"

"Lias, when I first met you, I was desperately hoping you were the one to fill the hole in my heart. Now I know you are. I will not force you, and I will not beg, nor will I coerce. You are free to take your time to make up your mind about the proposal, even if it takes twenty years or longer. Just as you are free to leave my castle with your children should you so desire. I place no hold on you. You are no longer my slave. You are my friend. But I would much rather you stay."

Lias didn't need to think about whether he would stay or go. "I would never leave you, Necromis. When I arrived here, I hated you. I hated everyone and everything. But my behavior toward you was undeserved. When you were sick, I begged for information from anyone who would speak to me. I have never been attracted to another man in my life, but you've shown me kindness when no one else wanted to even look at me." He smiled. "That is why I am here now, why I would rather spend my life with you than anyone else. I'm not ready to say yes to your offer of marriage, but I'm not going to say no, either. Just... give me time."

Necromis smiled at him. "Your love is all I truly need."

"You have it," Lias whispered and realized he meant it. And not merely the love of a friend or brother, but... love. Deep, romantic love for the man who had saved himself and his children.

Then something from the deep woods behind the manor house released a scream of pure rage and hate. The late evening sky darkened, and a storm suddenly blew up, turning all to blackness.

Necromis smiled coldly. "I beat you, you bastard," he whispered to the thing in the woods. "I beat you fairly on your own terms using your rules, and you can't stand it, can you?"

"Daddy?" asked Sunni, fear in her voice.

Lias froze, but he didn't take his gaze off of Necromis. "Girls, why don't you find Rufus, the horse, and say hello?"

Horses were always good for distracting little girls. When the children were gone, Lias turned and faced Necromis. The wind battered the windows, and lightning flashed, reflecting in Necromis' eyes. Lias glanced back at the window, where Necromis stared toward the forest, then back at Necromis.

"What is that?" Fear began twisting Lias' heart into knots. "*Who* did you beat?"

Necromis looked to him, as if wondering what to say. Then he drew Lias against his chest and held him close. "Just a lying monster. I love you Lias, that's all that matters. I am free now to love and get well and be the man you deserve."

Lias managed to get loose and put distance between them. He stared Necromis in the eye. He knew the answer before he even asked the question, but he had to hear it from Necromis.

"*Who*? I love you, too. But that doesn't mean I don't expect the truth. Khaylin the mage told me you were probably trying to break a curse. Who cursed you?"

Necromis looked as if he had been shot in the guts. "Lias, my love… I cannot lose you. Not when I have found you. Not when I have bound my heart and soul to you…"

It dawned on Lias that Necromis actually *feared* Lias would leave. Lias cupped Necromis' face between both hands. "I made a promise. I always keep my promises. I love you. I would love you whether you were a man or a woman. I love you because of the things that make you who you are." He studied Necromis' face, saw genuine fear in the man's eyes. "I will not leave you. Just tell me true: is Bonecracker the one you beat?"

Necromis broke utterly. "I could not lie, *would* not lie, to you, especially since I know Bonecracker too well. If I lied or told half-truths, Bonecracker would make sure you learned the truth about every hateful thing I had done."

So he told the truth—all of it. He had become monstrous to save the life of the man he loved, falling prey to a demon's trickery. He had murdered. He had eaten the flesh of his victims. He had rolled in their blood and fed their bones to a demon. All for the love of a stable boy.

Lias listened, half horrified and half sympathetic. "If I were a lesser man, I would let the demon have you," he said finally. "But I am not. Since my capture, I have done things of which I am not proud. Things that no civilized soul should ever do. I did them for my ex-wife in my quest to find her." He shook his head. "Am I disturbed by what you've told me? Yes. Any sane man would be. But it doesn't change how I feel about you. I have but one question: is it over?"

"For me, it is," said Necromis. "Bonecracker laid down the rules for my redemption himself. I met them. He cannot now cry foul. I have learned the ways of demons over the past years, Lias. They can twist things to their own advantages, but they cannot go back on their word. To do so would be a sin above all sins within their world. That is why he rages now and, like as not, is mocked by his hellish peers. I have defeated him, but I will not push my luck with him. I do not have to like a demon to have great respect for his power."

Lias nodded. After things he'd seen here—the nursemaid, the duppy—he knew how serious such matters could be. "No more killing," he said. "Promise me you are done with Bonecracker and any other demons... and I will marry you."

"I swear to you on the life you gave back to me that there shall be no more demons, save for the ones I must meet on the battlefield. No more murders, no more darkness, no more secrets and lies. No more blood rites. No more... Oh, poo, I'll have to give Ursine back. He's the only thing I liked about the curse."

119

One eyebrow raising, Lias stared at his lover and sighed. "Do I really want to know?"

"Well, he's... this half-bear, half-man undead, and he's not attractive in the least. I will really miss his raspberry tarts."

Lias groaned. "No. I really wish I hadn't asked," he muttered. "Now I'm going to have nightmares."

"Would you like to meet him?" asked Necromis brightly.

Lias took a deep breath. "He has been a part of your life for quite some time, and I wish to know you better. But if he is as... unappealing as you say in his appearance, then I would prefer to do it after we have eaten. That way, should my dinner make a resurgence, then it will be far less painful in the long run."

"Quite understandable, my beauty! Quite understandable. Now..." Necromis drew him close. "Perhaps what we need now is a lesson on how to make love in the bath..."

The door suddenly blew open, and there stood something that could only be called a nightmare. Lias took one look at the thing and screamed.

"Master! Master, do not send Ursine away! Please! Other masters so mean! I can be good and helpful! Please let Ursine stay!"

"Or not," said Necromis.

Lias fell backward, splashing water over the edge of the tub. Heart pounding, he stared at the... creature. He had no words to describe such a thing beyond a 'walking, talking abomination.' He looked at Necromis. "Ursine, I presume?"

"Ursine, this is my lover Lias. Lias, this is Ursine, who will resume speaking properly this instant. I do not have servants who speak gibberish."

Ursine immediately corrected himself. "Yes, Master, of course. Hello, Lias. My name is Ursine! Master, please do not send me away!"

"Ursine... what are you doing out of the chamber?"

"Chamber go bye-bye."

"What was that?"

"The chamber has vanished, my lord."

"Yes, I rather suppose it would. All right, take yourself to the high room on the fourth floor you like so much."

"Thank you, Master!" Ursine fled the room.

Necromis sighed heavily. "A lock is in order, I think."

Lias wasn't sure what to make of Ursine or the exchange he'd just witnessed. "He is... a demon? Is he harmless? Will the girls be safe with him here?"

"No, he's not a demon at all," said Necromis. "I'm not entirely certain what he *is*, but you have my word that he is harmless as a lamb. We will have to find a way to make his outsides match his insides." He looked at Lias, green eyes soft. "I am so sorry, Lias. Sorry I could not be truthful sooner. I needed to win your love, and I did not know how to do that and reveal all that I had become as well. I am still fearful you will leave."

Lias tipped his lover's head back a little and kissed him gently. "You are forgiven. I will not leave you."

Necromis returned the kiss. "Perhaps someday you will consider taking me inside of you. If not... I would indeed enjoy having you inside me. Very, very much."

They almost kissed. Almost. Then the door burst open, and in stormed a very angry woman.

Necromis sighed. "We shall have to fuck later. I defeated *my* demon. Here's *yours*."

Merdine stormed into the room in a rage. "How dare you treat me so shame... ful... ly..." her words slowed as she realized her former husband was naked in the bath with another man.

Lias rose and got out of the tub. Dripping wet and naked as the day he was born, he stalked over to her and pointed an accusing finger directly at her.

"You're naked!" she stated, trying to be horrified.

"Yes, I am because I want you to see every damn mark on my body. I was reduced to a subhuman monster

121

because of you! Because of your lies and tricks and, yes, I do believe you murdered Elyssa. You can play the dainty maid all you like, but I went through the bowels of the underworld trying to save you. Only to find you are a liar and likely a murderer as well," he snarled. "It is because of your treachery that I have spent the past year and a half in the worst hell you could never begin to imagine. I have been beaten, starved, raped, whipped, broken, bruised, bloodied—all because I thought to rescue you. You stole my children and my life. If you ever step foot near my girls, myself, or Necromis, I will make you wish you had never been born. I have far more important matters to attend to than to look at a used and discarded piece of rubbish."

"I am going nowhere without my children," she snarled. "And there are laws against what you are doing, you loathsome pig. I'll report you."

It was Necromis who spoke next, still weak, but it was clear that the ending of the curse had improved his strength.

"You are in Ixander, my lady," Necromis warned. "He can plough my fields at high noon on the lawns of the king, and, apart from attracting an audience and educating the masses, we will have broken no laws. Besides, sadly, we haven't done anything yet."

Lias balled his hands into fists. He'd never hit a woman, but Merdine was quickly testing his morality in such regards. "Get. Out. They are *my* children. You have no claim on them and nothing to stand on in this realm." He smiled, though there was no friendliness in it. "You might want to count yourself lucky I have not pursued charges of adultery, fraud, and kidnapping."

"I have no idea what you are talking about," she said dismissively. "And this is not over. I'll go to the king himself!"

"Oh, do tell Father I said hello," said Necromis. The knight began carefully easing himself out of the bath.

Lias hid his surprise and just smirked. "Leave." He backed her out the door. "While you still can." He slammed the door in her face and fell back against it. "Father?" he inquired.

"Not by blood, no, but in the last war, he lost all his children. For some reason, the dear man and his good wife like me, so when he passes from this earth in thirty or forty years peacefully in his sleep with a cat on his knees, I shall be king."

Lias helped Necromis out of the bath and over to the bed, then lay down beside him. "How are you feeling?"

"Better. As if a great weight has left and a lump of poison is no longer within me. Oh, Lias, I have done such horrendous things. I am sorry about the beating I gave you. I had no right."

"No," said Lias, "but I suspect it had more to do with the demon within you than your own free will."

"There may be some truth to that. Still..." He sighed quietly. "It shall be a long time ere I am at peace with myself."

Lias reached out to take his hands as they lay together, each sick and exhausted. Lias moved closer to Necromis and kissed him.

"We have to take things slow," said Lias. "I'm not too badly off, but you look as if you are made of glass."

"I am," said Necromis. "Glass and sadness. But do not concern yourself with me. Go see those children you destroyed yourself for."

"You're sure? You're not going to die on me, are you?"

Necromis opened his mouth, tried to think of something to say, then sighed. "I can't even think of a filthy joke. No, I shall not die. I have far too much to live for now."

Lias kissed him gently. "As do I. Though I do ask you request an end to people calling me the poo-flinger and other such terms."

"Consider it done."

They gazed at each other. Slowly, a grin spread over Lias' face. "Such a strange world we live in that it should bring me here."

123

They kissed, hands gently touching one another, Lias carefully exploring Necromis' wasted frame. He was so thin, so fragile. But he had seemed to gain a little strength now that Bonecracker was no longer crushing the life out of him. However, there were still so many questions. If Lias fell out of love with him, would the demon come back for the knight? There would be many conversations, but for now... rest.

The door slammed open yet again, and in thundered four little girls, Hawthorne's daughter having joined the herd.

Necromis winced at all the shrieking. "Lias, be a dear and have someone come up and install a lock, please, the sooner the better."

Then a veritable roaring lion of a man entered the room. Blassard was, by no means, back to his robust self, but he clearly felt much better than he had in ages.

"Uncle is feeling well again. What's for supper?"

"Lock," said Necromis.

Lias laughed. "See what woes you brought upon yourself!"

Necromis grudgingly sat up. "I'm not going down to dinner until I am dressed. Blassard, the ladies are under your care until such time as I am able to walk to the dining hall."

"Of course, of course. Come along, wee ones, and I shall tell you the tale of the dragon stuck on a hill."

Lias kissed Necromis as the group left. "Are you certain you wish to go to the dining hall?"

Necromis nodded. "I have found love, I am free of my curse, and Blassard is recovering. It is a night to celebrate."

Chapter Eight

Sunni, Elderwyn, and Karda were very impressed with Necromis' dining hall. It was done in blues and golds, with friezes of women running with wild horses and stags in a wood. The table seemed to go on forever, and the five of them gathered at one end was almost silly.

Although he had been invited, Blassard had opted instead to let Hawthorne examine him because he was supposed to be dying, not up telling tales. Not that anyone was complaining about this strange turn of events. Lias wondered if this, too, was part of the now-broken curse. Necromis, meanwhile, watched the three little girls eat like wild things with amusement.

"So I see your Daddy taught you the finest manners."

Lias chuckled. "I assure you that they were not raised in a barn. A cabin, yes. Barn, no. Girls, manners, please."

Elderwyn and Karda toned down their rambunctiousness and acted more like little ladies. Sunni, however, grinned, her mouth full of food. Lias spied a bit of gravy on her chin and, somehow, above her left eyebrow. He sighed.

"Well, it's a start, I suppose."

"We can hire them a proper nanny," said Necromis. "One approved by you, naturally. Someone to educate them in all ways, including... how to handle a spoon."

"Uh-oh!" said Sunni as her golden spoon somehow magically took flight.

Lias groaned, palm covering his eyes. "Yes. Please."

"I'll get it," Karda said. She retrieved Sunni's spoon.

Sunni giggled. "What do we call your boyfriend, Daddy?"

Had children always possessed this ability to mortify their parents? Lias peered at Necromis from between his fingers. "Any suggestions would be greatly appreciated."

"Well, I think 'Daddy' at this point is asking too much, and 'Uncle' is creepy… so I will say, for now, 'Necromis' will do until we get things properly sorted."

Elderwyn looked to her father. "Daddy, we don't ever have to live with Stepmother again, do we? Ever since the night you left, she's been horrid."

Lias smiled. "No, sweetheart. You will never have to live with her again. You're home with us, where you belong." Though he almost didn't want to know, he had to ask. "How was she horrid?"

"She kept talking about who we were going to marry and when, and told me I had to get married next summer when I turned thirteen to this old fat man who smelled. I said I didn't want to, and she said that did not matter. He was paying the highest bride-price."

Lias gritted his teeth, fury welling up inside him. "*No* daughter of mine will marry so young, and when she is ready, she will marry the one *she* chooses. I would never force any of you into such a thing. You're safe here." He glanced at Necromis. "There has to be something we can do. Merdine *will* find a way to retaliate. Though in the past, I was blind to her malevolence, recent events have shown me there is not evil to which she will not stoop."

"That is not a problem," said Necromis. "I have standing, I have guards, I have wealth. If she tries to take the children or harm them, I can retaliate as well. I'm sure she will not like my dungeons at all."

"Do you have monsters down there?" asked Sunni.

"Right now, all I have is a cantankerous old man who seems to think stealing and eating other people's horses is acceptable behaviour."

Lias snorted and prayed Ursine stayed wherever Necromis had sent him. The last thing the girls needed was to see… that. "Merdine likes to think she has standing when she does not. She was the midwife who delivered the girls, and she cared for my first wife during the awful illness that eventually took her life." Lias thought on it for a moment and grimaced. "Given that the illness was never named, a part of me wonders if perhaps Merdine had something to do with it."

"It is a common game," said Necromis. "Ingratiate oneself into the family, then kill the wife in order to claim the marriage bed. Your wife was a lady of quality and standing. I fear you have had a very cruel trick played upon you, Lias."

Lias nodded. "Having discovered her true nature, I would agree." Something thumped against the table repeatedly. Lias leaned down, sighed, and straightened back up. "Sunni, sweetheart, please don't kick the table leg."

Sunni stopped swinging her legs and blinked at him, eyes wide and gravy somehow stuck in her hair this time. "Can we have a puppy?"

Necromis' eyes became bright at the question, and without a word, he gestured to a servant, who ran out of the dining hall. The man returned in minutes with a truly gigantic puppy. It was so large that one first assumed it was an adult, but upon closer inspection, it proved to be just a clumsy baby dog. It was a deep chocolate brown, with long flappy ears, long flappy lips, and paws the size of plates.

"Does this suit you, my lady?"

Sunni squealed and jumped off her chair. She ran to the puppy and threw her arms around it, squishing the poor thing. Her sisters quickly joined her.

Lias stared at Necromis. "How...?"

Necromis smiled. "From my kennels. He was stepped on by a horse, and though he has mended, he will never be able to perform the duties for which he was bred. We were considering having him destroyed, but this seems a better fate to me."

Although Lias wondered what other ways his lover could eventually spoil the girls, he was still grateful. He got up and went to Necromis, kissing him. "Thank you," he said.

"Thank you, Necromis!" Sunni yelled.

The dog bowled her over, and she giggled. Within seconds, there was nothing but a giggling, squealing, panting, barking pile of fur and dresses on the dining room floor. Lias shook his head. Necromis stroked his hair, then kissed him.

"Forgive me, my love, for all the ugly things I have done. I was so blinded by my grief that I did not think and was too naïve to understand anyway. If it helps at all... I slew no innocents."

Lias rested his forehead on Necromis' and smiled. "I already forgave you. I did terrible things, too. I've said things to you that I never should have. I am sorry. I know you now, and none of them are true."

Necromis smiled faintly. "Well, they are a little true."

"Are you gonna have another baby when you get married?" Sunni asked her father.

Necromis gave Lias a truly wicked and toothy grin that can only be learned by a man who spent time enslaved by a demon. "There are spells. And you'd be *so* cute..."

"Oh, no," Lias laughed. "No. If anyone has to carry it, it will be you."

"Me? And ruin my lovely figure?"

Lias leaned down to Necromis' ear and whispered, "Just imagine the fun in getting that way."

Necromis gave him the same wicked look. "Let's not start something in front of the children we can't finish..."

Suddenly... the roaring, violent storm stopped. It was so abrupt, it was like slamming a door.

Necromis looked somewhat concerned. "Why did the storm end so suddenly?"

Lias approached one of the large windows. He peered outside. "It's still, quiet. Too quiet." He looked back at Necromis. "What's going on?"

Necromis shook his head. "I do not know. But we are safe here. I think it is time you got your daughters into a bath and found them a room."

"Shall I summon Sir Hawthorne and have the guards assembled?" asked the servant who had brought the puppy.

Necromis nodded, still fragile, but more than capable of running his castle. "Yes, thank you, Arin."

The servant departed.

Lias left the window and clapped his hands. "Okay, ladies. Time for washing and bed." The girls groaned in unison, but Lias shook his head. "There will be none of that. Let's find Merrigale and see if she can help you." He looked at Necromis. "Will you be all right if I am gone for a few minutes?"

"I'll be fine, Lias. I shall just be very slow and careful."

Merrigale was only too happy to help, as were a number of other servants, and even one of the slaves. The children each had their very own painted porcelain bath, filled with hot water and bubbles, with flower petals on the surface, and clean towels. No shared basin and cloth here.

Lias left his daughters to their privacy and found a couple of servants readying their room. He stepped in and helped them. "This room is larger than our entire cabin. The girls won't know what to do. This shared bed alone is four times larger than the one of the beds each girl had in the cabin."

"Well, we never thought the master would have children," said Merrigale, breathless with excitement. "Now there are three wee ladies! Oh, and here is Bruno. The master asked he watch over the little ladies tonight, and tomorrow, we shall set up proper shifts for the children's guards."

Bruno was the size of a mountain, with massive thighs and shoulders, clad in armor. He was huge and bearded and brawny and would daunt well-nigh anyone seeking to inflict harm. Lias could not help but notice the faint outline of a cylindrical nature that travelled far down his leg. It was camouflaged beneath his breeches, but... not quite enough. Bruno had been referred to once by Necromis as a "favourite."

Never in his life had Lias felt as... inadequate... as he did now. He discreetly glanced down at his own endowment. If there were spells in the library to enable a man to get pregnant, perhaps there were 'other' spells as well. He cleared his throat and looked back up, only to find Bruno watching him with a rather coy smirk.

"Yes. Well." Lias stood a bit straighter. "I'm sure Bruno will do nicely. Once he puts on a longer tunic."

"Never has the master been disappointed with my services," said Bruno, looking smug.

Lias marched over to the servant and said through gritted teeth, "Yes, well, tonight, you are minding my children, not fucking my fiancé. So dress accordingly."

Bruno could have ended Lias without a thought, but instead, he backed down. "Of course, forgive me. I meant no disrespect. I... I... I shall walk your puppy while the ladies bathe. Yes. I shall do that."

Bruno left with the puppy. Squeals echoed from the room where the girls were bathing. A moment later, one of the women helping the girls entered the bedroom, her clothing soaked to the bone. But her smile brightened up the entire room.

"I see you've met Sunni," Lias said, laughing.

"Such a delight to have children here!" she said. "Never have there been children here! And none born to any staff, how odd! It's almost as if this place had been under a curse!"

Lias kept his mouth shut on the curse bit. He didn't know what or how much the others knew about Necromis' dealings. "They will certainly bring a new level of insanity to this place," he laughed.

The puppy came galumphing back, tongue flying, being goofy as only an enormous puppy can. Bruno was right behind him, trying to catch him. Then, somehow, the playful beast grabbed his breeches and tore them off, running away with the prize, leaving Bruno on "full display," as it were, before Lias and the servants. Bruno did indeed possess the most formidable lance in the kingdom.

Lias' eyes widened, but he managed snap his mouth shut before his jaw could hit the floor. "No wonder Necromis preferred you," he muttered. When he heard the girls chattering, he grabbed an extra blanket off the bed and tossed it to Bruno. "Please…"

Bruno accepted the blanket gratefully, then fled the room once more to dress himself, Merrigale and her fellow maids giggling and tittering.

Then Necromis came up behind Lias, wrapping his arms around him. "I shall miss poor Bruno a little," said Necromis, purring. "Well. Parts of him."

Lias chuckled. "If you have an enlargement spell hiding in the library somewhere, I'm willing to try it."

"I not only have one, my precious gem, I can work it. I actually always wanted to be a wizard but past the neophyte spells and a few low-level ones, I have no talent for it. I can work glamours, though. After the wee ladies are a-bed, I shall grant you a prick that would shock my horse."

Lias laughed. "Now I am greatly intrigued."

The girls bounded into the bedroom, bathed and dressed for bed. They all skidded to a stop and stared, their mouths gaping open.

"We could fit our whole house in here!" Karda exclaimed.

"And all for you," said Necromis. "Bruno shall be outside the door all night to keep you safe. He's a very nice man and very strong. If you get scared, he will come chase away whatever frightens you."

Bruno, properly dressed once more, nodded firmly. He took up his position outside the door after the children were in bed.

Necromis led Lias away down the hall and whispered to him, "So what filthy debaucheries would you like to do to me tonight?"

Lias grinned. "I seem to recall you saying something about an enlargement spell…"

Necromis made a faint sound of anticipation. "Perhaps a few ropes thrown in for good measure?"

"Mmm… the notion of you at my mercy is quite enticing." Lias stopped walking and backed Necromis up against the wall but gently, mindful of his fragility. And his own, for that matter. "Perhaps something over your eyes as well? So you have no idea what I'm doing until I do it."

"No ice cubes!" stated Necromis. "I hate getting ice on me!"

"I promise: no ice. Any other big no-nos?"

"No cake frosting and large dogs, either. Honestly, you have no idea what some people consider humorous. Having someone smear me with food and then letting a dog the size of a mountain lick it off is not my idea of a good time."

"A dog?" Lias shuddered. "No... I'm the only one who does the licking." He took Necromis' arm and led him to the bedroom.

"I must say you've corrupted wonderfully." Necromis shut the door after them as they entered the bedroom, then turned the new lock. He turned to Lias and slipped his arms around him, kissing him. "Now how can I keep you away from all those other men and women who must want you?"

Lias kissed him. "You don't have to do anything to keep them away. They are invisible to me. As likely I am to them."

"Oh, hush."

Lias walked them to the bed, helping Necromis down to the mattress. "I understand now why Merdine claimed to love me but did not seem to enjoy being with me. No doubt my touch disgusted her. You, however, want me to love you, to pleasure you."

"With all my filthy little heart."

Lias grabbed Necromis' wrists and gently pinned them to bed before kissing the man hard. Play would be nowhere near as hard as Necromis might like; the knight was too fragile and Lias too inexperienced.

"Perhaps, just for our first time, we shall forgo the ropes and spell."

"Yes, well, there is wisdom in your suggestion," Necromis said breathlessly. "Oh, Lias... take me hard and deep. Bend me to your will. Ride me like a bad borrowed pony!"

"You're insane," Lias laughed.

"Oh, dear one, did you just only now notice?"

Lias smiled. "What do you need me to do?"

"Well, I was rather hoping you would catch me, subdue me, bind me, then, doing your best Evil Mage impression, read the scroll of enlargement before violating my innocent virginal personage. Preferably without laughing your head off."

Lias smiled slowly. "I could chase you."

Necromis' eyes glittered with anticipation, and he tried very hard to do as ordered, apparently forgetting that he was in no fit state to run anywhere. He swore as, when trying to take his second step, his knees gave way, and he fell to the floor, Lias catching him.

"Well, I suppose you weren't expecting to catch me quite so easily," he quipped, leaning forward for a kiss.

Lias wrapped his arms around Necromis and helped him to stand before he carried him back to the bed, placing him on it.

"Probably for the best," he said. As he spoke, he moved forward to straddle Necromis' torso. "Neither of us are in any fit state to run anywhere, and trying to do so would only use up strength and energy better saved for other things."

"Quite agreed."

Lias bent to kiss Necromis, reaching up to run his fingers through the long white hair. He was so fragile. What would this be like when Necromis was restored to full health? He was a very large, powerful man when well. Lias found himself a little intimidated by the thought, but by then... should he have not become to used to him?

Necromis returned the kiss. "Lias, I love you. I had not realized how much of my life had been lost in pain, anger, and resentment. I had lost my freedom and my love, so decided to revel in debauchery instead. But you now are my only love."

Lias smiled. "I know. I love you, too. I never expected to say such a thing to another man, much less touch one as I have you. But you are different than anyone I've ever known."

"You are a little like another I knew," said Necromis softly, faded green eyes touched with sadness. "But not enough to be anyone but Lias to me."

"Careful," Lias said, smiling. "You may ruin your fearsome reputation should anyone know you're a romantic man at heart."

"Alas, they know of my shame. I am undone."

Lias smiled, then eased himself down beside Necromis. There would be plenty of nights for raucous sex, but it would not be this night. Tonight was for first times and gentleness, for exploration and learning. Lias had no doubt that in the days to come he would come to know all of this man's quirks.

The world was unnaturally still now that the storm had ceased, and Lias found himself wishing for sounds of any type. But it was growing late, and all others were asleep. Lias gently explored Necromis' wasted frame, wincing at how frail the other man was.

"Are you sure you wish for me to continue?"

"I very much do. I'm stronger now that the curse is broken. Just… take care with me."

Lias nodded. As Necromis relaxed and closed his eyes, tangling his hands into Lias' hair, Lias began gently kissing his way down Necromis' long body, finally encountering a stiff penis. He didn't let himself think about what he was about to do because he was a little afraid he wouldn't have the nerve. He took it into his mouth, closing his eyes, thinking the stiff cock tasted faintly like Necromis' floral soap. Definitely not the worst thing he had ever had in his mouth. He smiled as he heard Necromis gasp.

"And where did you learn this delightful trick?"

Lias raised his head. "My first wife."

"And where, pray tell, did *she* learn it?"

"I never wanted to think about that…"

"Quite."

Lias continued to explore Necromis, touching his hips, thighs, and then reaching up to his waist. He flushed nervously as Necromis drew up one long leg in an obvious invitation and slowly dared to reach down between the lean buttocks, finding and touching his tight hole. He enjoyed the purrs and moans from his lover, but this was all very strange. He raised his head once more.

"Are you sure you wish me to do this?"

"You're so delightfully innocent! Just to be clear, my dear one, and to reiterate my previous statement, ride me like a bad rented pony."

"As you request, sire, I live to serve."

"I'm not 'sire' yet, dear one. The king still lives. Here." Necromis reached for a small bottle of oil that stood on the nightstand. "You will want this."

Lias accepted it. "Just so you know, I fully anticipate being terrible at this."

Necromis giggled, a full nose-wrinkling giggle. "Ah, Lias, you are a gift to my dark heart. So be terrible. It will not matter when we have a lifetime to educate you."

Lias smiled, then opened the bottle to pour some oil on himself. Then he used his slick fingers to gently stroke Necromis' anus.

"Let me know if I'm just making a mess of things."

Necromis' eyes were closed, and he was breathing slightly harder now. "So far, all is well."

Lias felt himself growing uncertain he would be able to perform this act, but he capped the oil and set the bottle aside. Mentally bracing himself, he carefully mounted his lover, who did not seem disappointed in the least.

"I'm not too heavy for you, I hope?"

"No. Not at all."

"I'm just worried…"

"Lias, do shut up."

They kissed, holding each other close as Lias began carefully thrusting. He had already scarred Necromis' face.

He could not imagine what the reaction would be if he somehow broke him.

Necromis nipped Lias' jaw, tangling his hands into the shaggy black mane that, like its defiant owner, had never been under full control. He drew his long legs up to wrap around Lias' waist.

"So gentle you are. I'd forgotten in all my debauchery how wonderful a light touch can be."

Lias kissed him, gently touching him. "Chamber pots aside, I could never hurt you."

"So if they once more become employed in battle, I am to consider the relationship over."

Lias laughed, then kissed him firmly, their tongues touching and exploring one another. There was only the sound of their breathing, small gasps, quiet cries, little exclamations. Then Lias heard Necromis' breathing become rough, and his cries become louder. His eyes were closed, his head flung back, white throat on full display. Unable to resist, Lias nipped the near-translucent flesh and winced as he felt Necromis' nails begin to claw at his back.

"Careful," he whispered.

Necromis said nothing in return, but his hands moved away from the still-tender scars. He began breathing more loudly, his cries becoming more intense. His passion demanded gripping his lover, but some part of his brain understood he could not do that, so he clamped down on Lias' biceps before screaming like one of the wild mountain cats. There was an immediate pounding at the door. Apparently, Hawthorne did not approve of his patients making strange screaming noises.

"Necromis! Are you all right?"

The knight's eyes opened, and Lias would swear they glowed like the emeralds mined by dwarfs to the far west.

"I'm fucking busy! And vice-versa!"

Lias heard Hawthorne sigh and mutter "Well, he certainly told me."

Necromis screamed again, and Lias felt wet heat on his stomach as his own pleasure reached its climax. He shuddered and cried out, spilling deep within Necromis' body. For a long perfect moment, everything around him stopped. Then he gasped and collapsed, utterly spent. He forced his weakened frame off of Necromis for fear of crushing him and collapsed beside him on the bed. They lay side by side, panting, as Necromis took Lias' hand.

"So, now you've had your first man."

"And likely my only. Was I a disappointment?"

"A little timid, but given our current condition, that was neither bad nor unexpected. Once we're both healthy, we can bring out the whips and chains and sock puppets."

Lias laughed and shook his head. "This I vow: to one night get you very drunk and ask you about all your escapades."

"I assure you that will take more than one night. Now let us have our wine in the bath, while we think of what food we would like to have brought up."

"Sounds perfect to me."

Lias got up and helped Necromis off the bed. He pulled a cord nearby and found robes to cover them both before servants came in to fill the bath. Hawthorne also arrived to grumble about block-headed patients up to nonsense, but Necromis just grinned.

Finally, Hawthorne looked his friend in the eye. "Tell me true, how do you feel?"

"Fucking fantastic."

"Necromis, there is something deeply wrong with you."

"You're right. The tub is not nearly large enough to include you in the bath."

Hawthorne sighed heavily, patting his friend on the head as if he were an exceptionally dense dog. Then he departed.

As soon as the water neared the top, but not enough to spill over once they were inside, Lias shut the bedroom door and held both glasses of wine while Necromis got into the water. Then Lias joined him, leaning back against his lover.

"I could stay right here for an eternity," Lias said.

"As could I. Tell me, do you think you will ever be willing to have me inside you, given what you have been through?"

"I am not saying no. I am saying at this time I think it unlikely. I've only just learned physical love with a man can be a lovely thing. I'd hate to have old memories destroy that."

"As would I. In that case, I ask only that you let me know if you decide to have me."

"Oh, that indeed I will do. But I am content with what we have."

"As am I, dear Lias. May it stay this way always."

* * *

Lias was gently nudged awake by a hand on his shoulder. The room was dark, save for the light of a few candles.

"Lias. Lias, the sun has not risen. The sky is black, and there are no stars above. Something is very wrong."

"What?" Lias sat up and immediately noted the look of sheer fright on Necromis' face. "Where are the girls?" He flung off the blanket and began dressing. "Sunni is terrified of the dark." He peered out of the shutters on the window, brow furrowing. "What is going on, Necromis?"

"I do not know. We are the only ones awake. I checked on the girls, but they will not be roused, nor anyone else. Bruno stands upright with eyes open at his post but sees and hears me not."

Fear shot through Lias. "Bonecracker. Could this be some sort of retaliation for us breaking the curse that bound you?"

"I am thinking it may be. Or perhaps something new. I am frightened, Lias. Have you any skill with a weapon?"

Lias finished dressing. "Do you have a woodsman's axe?"

138

"Nay." Necromis hurried as quickly as his weakened frame would allow across the room to a cupboard that Lias had never realized was indeed a cupboard. He opened it and brought out a well-crafted, medium sized battleaxe, showing it to Lias. "Will this do?"

Lias took the axe, stepped back, and swung it as if chopping a tree. He nodded. "It will. I've never fought anything like what may await us, Necromis. What else could this be if not Bonecracker?"

"It will not be Bonecracker. It will be a minion. Bonecracker does not risk his own neck. Battle is not his forté. Deception, lies, and misinformation are his..." Necromis paused as he saw Ursine standing in the doorway, gazing at him. "Oh, Ursine, tell me that you are not part of this."

"Me? No, Master. I came because I wanted to know why the sun is not up. I can awaken no one!"

"But who..." Lias worried his lower lip for a moment before continuing. "The nursemaid, the one who tormented me. Was she one of Bonecracker's minions? Could she be behind this?" Quick on the heels of that thought came another. "Why would Bonecracker — or any minion of his — show now? We broke the curse. Didn't we?"

"I do not believe this is the work of the nursemaid," said Necromis. "I believe this is the work of a selfish, greedy woman and her selfish, greedy husband. Ursine, stand guard over the children. Blood will spill before this passes."

"Merdine," Lias snarled, fury surging through him. He approached Necromis. "Never have I raised my hand to a woman, but I will *kill* her — and anyone working with her — should she lay a finger on my children."

Ursine lumbered off to the children's room to look after them, leaving Lias and Necromis standing in the darkness. Lias could hear him breathing as he lit another candle.

"Necromis, you are so frail. I don't want you in battle."

Necromis had a hand against his heart, and he seemed weaker than he had before. "On my nightstand there is a clear potion with a pearl in it. Bring it."

Lias did, but he wasn't happy with the idea of his lover in a fight. Necromis drank the potion, pearl and all, then tossed the bottle onto the bed. Within moments, he was clearly a great deal stronger.

"Stay close to me," said Necromis. "We do not know what is out there."

"And what, pray tell, was that, my love?"

Necromis just grinned. "A potion of strength and stamina, and if I have to tell you why I should want one, then I truly do despair. Stay close."

Lias nodded and adjusted his grip on the axe. "I'll follow your lead."

He fell into step with Necromis as they started out into the dark hallway. There was no light anywhere—inside or out. Only a strange gloom that permitted them just enough brightness to see. He shoved down the fear for the girls' safety, but he prayed Ursine guarded them well. He also prayed the girls didn't wake to find the grotesque creature standing watch. Necromis seemed to sense Lias' thoughts.

"He has no great magic, but some minor spells I taught him. If the girls awaken, they will find only a large bear. Granted, it's frightening enough, but not as frightening as poor Ursine."

Relieved, Lias focused on the matter at hand. "At least our girls will be safe," he said. "Where are we going?"

"Our girls?"

"I'll keep them if you don't want to share."

"No, I am more than happy to share, my love."

Necromis paused, looking out the window at the great fire blazing in the distance, showing the faint outline of a temple. "He dares us to come to him, but we will not. The true danger is in this house. We will go to the cellars and dungeons and work our way up."

Lias shuddered. The fact that danger lurked in here — in their *home* — made fresh anger swell to the surface. He gripped the axe tighter. "He will pay for this."

Necromis shook his head. "It is not Bonecracker. He did not go to her. She went to him. Bonecracker is but the weapon. Your former wife is the assailant. There is no point in wasting our wrath on Bonecracker. He, at least, keeps his word."

"So do I," Lias growled under his breath. "I will tear her apart for this."

They slipped down the long flight of stairs into the depths of the castle. There were no prisoners being held there, save for the horse-eater, who was likewise in a deep trance, which was not surprising considering what Necromis had been doing with them. But then… they saw movement within a cell.

"Come forth!" shouted Necromis. "Come forth and show yourself!"

A slender figure appeared, face gaunt, eyes lifeless, the long hair dirty and tied back with a leather string. He was clad as a stable boy, and the way Necromis froze and began to shake told Lias this could only be Sterling.

"Oh, gods," Lias muttered. He squeezed Necromis' shoulder gently. What kind of cruel, sick joke was this? Lias watched as his lover seemed to crumble inside, and he wished there was something he could do. *Is… this real?" Is* he *real?* Lias wanted to ask, but he didn't.

Necromis dropped his sword, and the two ran to each other, embracing, weeping, sinking to the straw-covered floor as they held one another.

"Are you real, dear one?" whispered Necromis. "Do my eyes see true? Show me a sign."

Sterling drew back to lower the front of his breeches just slightly, showing a small scar that Necromis clearly recognized.

"By all the gods, it is you. But how…?"

"A woman I do not know went to Bonecracker," said Sterling. "She made a terrible, terrible bargain, meant

141

only to hurt you and a man called Lias. You see… you must choose. If you keep me, Lias dies. If you keep Lias, I die. If you keep us both, three children die. The woman seeks only to hurt Lias, but Bonecracker seeks to hurt *you*. This woman has become a bride to the demon and vowed to satisfy all its whims in return for this. Kinwill, I am at a loss as to what to do…"

Ice seeped into Lias' veins. The axe clattered to the floor. How could he ever compete with Necromis' first love? Lias thought of his girls, of how he would never see them grow up, become the strong women he knew they would be. He closed his eyes and leaned back against the nearest wall, the strength leeched from his body.

Merdine had outplayed them. He swore he would haunt her until the end of time for this. He opened his eyes and watched Necromis and Sterling. It felt as if he'd already died and simply observed the reunion as a spirit, unable to tell Necromis how much he loved him.

"Hush, my little darling one," said Necromis, softly kissing Sterling. "There is a way to save you both and the babies, too. I see now what I must do."

Necromis helped Sterling up and led him by the hand to Lias. "Sterling, this is Lias, the man who brought love back to my heart after I lost you. Lias, this is the man who taught me what real love is. If either of you feel anything for me at all, you will love one another as I have loved you, and tell the children of me, so they do not forget. For I will not choose. I will simply give Bonecracker what he desired all along."

"What!" Lias grabbed Necromis' shoulders and shook the man hard. "Have you lost your mind? I will *not* allow this!"

Necromis gazed at him. "Lias, how can I choose? Tell me: which of your children would you sacrifice? Could you make that decision? Or would you give yourself instead?"

"I would. Sterling was here long before me. All I ask is that you care for my babies. I love you. I can't live without you now."

"No," said Necromis, with the sort of finality that meant he would hear no more. Lias and Sterling were suddenly pushed into a cell, and the door locked after them. Necromis then hung the key up out of reach of their hands. "No. My time has ended here. I have spilled too much blood. I will spill no more, and I will not take a father from a child. Sterling, my darling one…" Necromis kissed him hard through the bars. "Be good to Lias. He has a head of iron, and he bites, but he will see you are cared for. All the deeds to the property are in my ironwood puzzle-box. Be well, my beauties. I love you both."

"Necromis!" Lias shouted, gripping the bars hard enough to bruise his hands. "Don't you *dare* do this!"

Necromis gazed at him for a long time, then stepped close and kissed him. "Goodbye, my Lias. Be happy. Look after Sterling."

Then he was gone, running up the stairs, his long white hair flying behind him. Unable to process what had just happened, Lias stared through the bars, his fingers still in a death grip around them. He finally pried himself away and began looking for some way out of the cell.

"There has to be… something," he muttered. He reached through the bars in hopes that maybe he could grab the key hanging nearby. He growled when it didn't work. "Damn it!"

Sterling was searching as well, clearly as frantic as Lias. "Dammit, why is this dungeon so clean? Who cleans a dungeon? Ah!" He pounced on something and held it out to Lias. It was a petrified rat tail. "You try. Your arms are longer."

Lias grabbed the tail and, holding the very end, extended his arm through the bars. The tail touched the key, setting the damn thing swinging on the hook. Lias grumbled and stretched as much as his arm would go. He got the tip of the tail through the key ring loop and lifted slowly.

"Got it!" He caught the key and unlocked the cell. "Come on!"

Sterling was slender and small, but he was wiry and strong. He shot up the stairs like an arrow, clearing two and three stairs at a time, his long brown ponytail swinging. He paused at the top of the stairs and looked back at Lias.

"Hurry!"

Lias caught up and shoved the door open. "Where did he go? Which way?"

"I do not know. I have been dead for eight years! I thought this was *your* castle!"

Lias snorted and grabbed Sterling's hand, dragging the man down the hall. "Not mine, but let's try this way."

They ran down the hall, then skidded to a stop. Lias recognized the main hall. He tugged Sterling toward the front door and grabbed the handle. The door swung open to a tempest raging outside. Lias shoved Sterling behind him to shield the smaller man from the swirling winds.

"Necromis!" he shouted into the rain and dark.

Sterling squirmed past him, screaming Necromis' former name, stopping a short distance ahead of Lias. "Kinwill! Kinwill, come back to me! To us! I don't care if I have to share you, just do not force me to live without you!"

Lias spotted fire in the distance. "This way!" He grabbed Sterling's hand and led the way into the forest, toward the fire.

They ran to the flame, but no matter how hard or how fast, the flame was always just out of reach, fluttering through the trees, taunting and eluding them. The faint sounds of a distant battle could be heard, and sometimes Necromis' voice, but it was hard to hear what he was saying. Then came a long, wailing scream, and then storm ceased. There was a deadly, hateful silence.

"No..." Lias barreled through the trees and skidded to a stop in a clearing. Not far away was Bonecracker's temple, though Lias hardly cared about that now. "No!" He fell to his knees beside Necromis' broken, bleeding body. "No. No, no, no. *You can't leave us like this!*"

"Oh, poor Lias. Poor Sterling. Is this not the way your romance was supposed to end?"

Lias looked up and screamed at the hideous thing he saw before him. It was like a pile of corpses, yet somehow alive, with three crushed and rotting heads that all spoke in unison. It smiled at him and began shuffling closer.

"Surely, you do not blame me. He *had* a choice, Lias. Is it my fault he chose to give himself to me? Now stand aside. I have waited a long time for these bones. I will enjoy them most..."

Lias did not know what made him reach for the pendant around his neck. All he knew was this beautiful man who had lost himself for love would not be turned into gnawed scraps by this monster. He tore it from around his neck and hurled it at the beast. When it hit the dead flesh, there was a hideous scream. The flesh burned and smoldered, and as Bonecracker tried to reach for it, the thing fell into his gaping ribcage. Shrieking mindlessly in pain that was beyond the imaginings of even the most battered mortal, Bonecracker fled into the woods.

Sterling came to stand beside Lias, resting a hand on his shoulder, looking around at the clearing. The temple had been here mere seconds ago. The smell of wood smoke hung in the air as the sun slowly appeared through the unnatural gloom Bonecracker had cast. Now there was no temple, no demon, and only a broken body on the ground, covered in mud and blood, his long white hair that had flowed like mercury ripped from his scalp.

Then, as they watched, a gigantic white bear made of pure light moved soundlessly into the clearing. It walked over to the body, then bent its gigantic head to lift him in its jaws. Somehow, it put Necromis across its own back, then turned and walked away in utter silence. Despite the evil he had done, the god he truly served had forgiven him. Lias moved to go after the bear, but Sterling caught his arm.

"He is gone," said Sterling hoarsely. "Let him go."

Lias stared at the ground in front of him where, only a moment ago, Necromis' broken body had been. Now there

145

was only a length of white hair that had been ripped from his scalp. Lias shook his head, not wanting to believe any of it.

"Why?" he whispered.

Sterling shook his head. "Why any of it? Why was I sold by a kind man to one known to be violent and cruel? Why was I denied the chance to be with a man who loved me? Why do we stand now with only blood in the dust and this grim token?"

Sterling picked up the length of hair from the ground as Lias stood slowly and approached Sterling. He ran his fingers over the hair.

"His love for you is what ultimately saved me." Lias looked at Sterling. He could see why Necromis had been in love with the young man. "I don't..." He shook his head and glanced around. "I don't know what to do."

"He wished for us to live," said Sterling. "To live and perhaps love one another, either as friends or more. He gave his life for us and the children. I say we see if we can honour that. Let us leave this place and return to the castle. Come."

Sterling linked his arm through Lias'.

Lias glanced around the clearing one more time before letting Sterling lead him away. "I don't understand. You were dead, weren't you?"

"I was, believe me. Dead and murdered and in the ground, sacrificed to Bonecracker as a sick joke to keep me out of the hands of the man who loved me. Then last night my bones were dragged out from under the temple, made to live again, and sent on a mission to torment someone I least wished to hurt. But the dead learn things, Lias. We do not lie as logs in the ground. We hear."

"He loved you so much," Lias said, glancing at Sterling. "More than anyone realized, I think."

"I loved him." Sterling said nothing more until they were well clear of the woods. Then he stopped and turned to look at the forest. He walked to a large rock and stepped onto it, Necromis' hair about his neck like a strange scarf. Then, as the sun rose high, Sterling's eyes narrowed.

"The dead hear things, Lias. Shall I show you what I heard as I lay under the temple and rotted and raged and hated, while monsters toyed with all I held dear?"

Lias was almost too leery to ask, but he nodded. "Yes. Please show me."

Sterling smiled. And it was not a nice smile. He raised his arms, letting the sun warm him, and began screaming words, freakish, guttural names that made the ground quiver and boom while the trees shook as if trying to flee. Sterling screamed the words one after another after another, and each time he did so, something shrieked in agony and a black cloud rose from the woods, stinking of rot and excrement. The final name felled some trees, and one great ancient oak tore itself free of its own roots as it tried to escape the sound of what Lias came to realize were names. Then all was silent. After a few moments, a bird warily tweeted, as if asking if the chaos was over. Sterling looked to Lias.

"I learned if you scream a demon's true name in the sunlight, you kill it. The trick is to get the name and speak it properly. For eight years, I listened very, very carefully, so that if ever my chance came, I would be ready."

Lias barely managed to think, let alone speak, after that display. "I wish I'd known such things." He reached for his pendant, then remembered he no longer had it. "It was my only defense against them when Necromis told me what it did. Why did you call him Kinwill?

"That was who he was when I knew him," said Sterling. "Kinwill the Stable Boy, who would borrow the horses of knights and lords, pick up a stick, and pretend to slay dragons. Kinwill, who wished to acquire elven horses to breed silver and golden mounts for lords and ladies and to earn enough money to buy me so we could spend our nights making love on a proper bed with a feather mattress."

Lias smiled. "I wish it would have happened that way. He was a wonderful man, and I still don't believe I

147

deserved him, given the things I said and did when he first bought me."

"Never question the good things, Lias. Just be grateful for them. They vanish all too quickly. That is why we must not waste the final gift he gave us: each other." Sterling took Lias' hand. "We must at the very least honour him with friendship. He begged us to look after one another."

Lias squeezed Sterling's hand gently. "Agreed." He sighed. "I need to check on the girls — hopefully, before Ursine scares them to death. Or... will Ursine still be here, if Necromis is gone?"

"What's an Ursine?"

Lias grimaced. "I'd forgotten..." How did he explain Ursine? "Ursine is... a... demon. I think. Not exactly the prettiest thing I've seen, but he has a heart of gold. Unfortunately... you can *see* his heart."

"Eew..." Sterling tripped and landed in the dust rather gracelessly. He gave Lias a chagrined look. "I'm a little weak I think."

Lias rushed to help him up, holding Sterling gently under the arms as he helped the man stand. Sterling felt light and delicate, and the young man's features were almost angelic. Lias realized exactly why Necromis — or anyone, for that matter — could fall for him. Sterling was beautiful.

"Are you all right? Are you hurt?"

Sterling brought a hand to his brow. "I don't know. After all that has transpired... I think..." Sterling fainted into a limp, albeit lovely, noodle.

Lias lifted him with very little effort. He held Sterling close to him and walked through the still-open front door. Lias thought he heard commotion upstairs, but he ignored it for the moment. He carried Sterling into a room that turned out to be some sort of parlor. He placed the young man on one of the couches and brushed a bit of hair from Sterling's face.

"No wonder he fell in love with you," Lias muttered.

148

"Daddy!" shouted Eldwyn. "There's a big fuzzy bear up here! And he's friendly! When's breakfast? Can the bear eat with us?"

Lias whirled around and caught Eldwyn. He buried his face in her soft hair. "You're safe. Oh, thank the gods. Where are your sisters?" He cupped her face. "Sweetie… Necromis. He's… gone."

She stared at him. She had not known Necromis long, but she had clearly become fond of him. She did not cry, but her eyes welled up with tears. "Gone where? Doesn't he like us anymore?"

Lias sighed tiredly. "No, he loved us more than I can explain to you right now. I will tell you all about it. Later."

Epilogue

Months had passed. The year had gone on, ended, then begun anew, travelling its normal path until it reached summer. Blassard had recovered and grew well and was now in line for the throne, with Hawthorne as his chosen advisor. Lias could bask in the warm weather, watching his daughters play and grow strong. They were in the garden now, a large, enclosed yard with more than enough room to play.

It was so very like the vision Lias had long ago, when Necromis forced him to eat the grey lichen. Rabbits played and scampered, and a great wolf, found as a pup in the winter and now half grown, drank cream from a pail as Sunni sat upon his back. There was peace here, and happiness, and in the center of all was a simple white monument to a man he had loved.

Someone sat beside him, and Lias glanced up to see it was Sterling. The two smiled at each other, each understanding one another's sadness.

"He would have wanted us to be happy, you know," said Sterling.

"I am," said Lias. "I just miss him so terribly."

"As do I," said Sterling.

They sat together, watching the children play. Then Sterling reached out to take Lias' hand. Lias smiled and turned his head to kiss Sterling's temple.

"I thought tonight… if you wanted to… you could sleep beside me."

Sterling smiled. "I'd like that."

ABOUT THE AUTHOR

Alyx Jae Shaw is a writer of sci-fi, fantasy, and horror for a primarily LGBTQT+ audience. Her current (and in her own opinion, BEST work), is Gryphons, which can be found on Amazon, and was attacked by a right wing hate group for reasons that cannot be determined, as they had clearly never read it. She lives in Abbotsford British Columbia with her two pet chickens. It is believed the chickens write the novels themselves using Alyx as a mind-controlled meat-bag. Alyx is fond of cooking, mead-making, drawing and painting, and talks a lot of smack for someone who once lost an entire unopened can of paint in a small apartment.

https://www.facebook.com/alyx.j.shaw